"Full of suspense, intrigue, and the twists and turns of true love, this is a story that will grip you from page one."
—ADRIANA TRIGIANI, author of *Lucia, Lucia*

"Loved it, loved it, loved it! Refreshingly romantic, dangerously good fun, hugely addictive...a pure pleasure to read...Intelligent, moving, and sweetly wise."
—JOANNE HARRIS, author of *Chocolat*

Praise for
THE DEATH AND LIFE OF CHARLIE ST. CLOUD

"*The Sixth Sense* meets *Field of Dreams* in this heartwarming, old-fashioned fable." —*Washington Post*

"[Sherwood] makes you believe—and that's miracle enough."
—*Newsweek*

"[An] emotionally satisfying work." —*Denver Post*

"A perfect miracle of a love story. Ben Sherwood is a dauntless writer, taking his readers on a really stunning, amazing ride. He breaks your heart and heals it, somehow at the same time. I found the novel to be almost unbearably wonderful." —Luanne Rice

"'Magical' and 'mystical' do justice to the book, but perhaps the adjective that best suits what Sherwood's book offers is 'transcendent.' In other words, I laughed, I cried, and I stayed up really late on a weeknight so I could finish the book in one sitting. *The Death and Life of Charlie St. Cloud* is that good." —*St. Louis Post-Dispatch*

"Sherwood is an effortless storyteller with a nice rhythm."
—*Washington Post Book World*

"Uniquely lyrical, Sherwood's story of a devotion so strong it transcends death is mystical, magical, and moving." —*Booklist*

"Sherwood steps into the pastoral landscape of Thornton Wilder's *Our Town* and Frank Capra's *It's a Wonderful Life* to explore the tortured lives of those who cannot let go and those who blame themselves for life's misfortunes....A modern-day O. Henry, Sherwood conjures the timeless muse of John Lennon to deliver the strongest ecumenical message our country could embrace in this post–September 11th era." —BookReporter.com

"A touching story of loss, love, and new beginnings."
—*Chattanooga Times Free Press*

"A rewarding and moving story about life, death, guilt, and the loss the living must both suffer and survive....It's fanciful, sad, and heartwarming all at the same time." —*Richmond Times-Dispatch*

"Entertaining." —*Dallas Morning News*

"A mystical and unforgettable story that will keep readers in suspense." —*Orlando Sentinel*

"Very provocative." —*Salt Lake City Deseret Morning News*

Praise for
THE MAN WHO ATE THE 747

"Magical, quirky, and gorgeously written...nothing short of mesmerizing." —*Entertainment Weekly*

"This one is a gem." —*Washington Post*

"Brilliantly written, a true love story with fabulous characters. A joy to read. A book you are not going to want to miss." —*New York Post*

"A moving love story with laughs." —*US Weekly*

"Delightful, warm, and quirky." —*Denver Post*

"The comic love story of the year." —*Tennessean*

"Ben Sherwood is a modern-day Mark Twain who writes of smalltown America with love, affection, and a definite twinkle in his eye. A delightful and surprising book from start to finish."
—Fannie Flagg, bestselling author of *Standing in the Rainbow*

"Hilarious and heartwarming." —*Chicago Tribune*

"A wonderfully wacky, wise, charming, and romantic satire, filled with lovably eccentric characters who know the secret of true love."
—*Kirkus Reviews* (starred review)

"A sweet, quirky novel." —*USA Today*

"Imaginative, tasty, and heartwarming. The book's charm and inherent sweetness win the day." —*People*

ALSO BY BEN SHERWOOD

The Man Who Ate the 747

BEN SHERWOOD

THE DEATH
AND LIFE
OF CHARLIE ST. CLOUD

BANTAM BOOKS

THE DEATH AND LIFE OF CHARLIE ST. CLOUD
A Bantam Book

PUBLISHING HISTORY
Bantam hardcover edition published March 2004
Bantam trade paperback edition / March 2005

Published by Bantam Dell
A Division of Random House, Inc.
New York, New York

The lines from "dive for dreams" copyright © 1952, 1980, 1991 by the Trustees for the E. E. Cummings Trust, from COMPLETE POEMS: 1904–1962 by E. E. Cummings, edited by George J. Firmage. Used by permission of Liveright Publishing Corporation.

Book design by Lynn Newmark
Art on title page © Royalty-Free/Corbis

Library of Congress Catalog Card Number: 2003057802

Bantam Books and the rooster colophon are registered trademarks of Random House, Inc.

ISBN 0-553-38325-6

Printed in the United States of America
Published simultaneously in Canada

www.bantamdell.com

BVG   10 9 8 7 6 5 4 3

*To Karen
and as always
the memory of Richard Sherwood*

We are not human beings having a spiritual experience;
we are spiritual beings having a human experience.

—PIERRE TEILHARD DE CHARDIN

There is a land of the living and a land of the dead
and the bridge is love, the only survival, the only meaning.

—THORNTON WILDER

INTRODUCTION

I BELIEVE IN MIRACLES.

Not just the simple wonders of creation, like my new son at home nursing in my wife's arms, or the majesties of nature, like the sun setting in the sky. I'm talking about real miracles, like turning water into wine or bringing the living back from the dead.

My name is Florio Ferrente. My father, a fireman, christened me after St. Florian, the patron saint of our profession. Like my pop, I worked my whole life for Engine Company 5 on Freeman Street in Revere, Massachusetts. I served as God's humble servant, going where the Lord dispatched me, saving the lives that He wanted rescued. You could say I was a man on a mission, and I'm proud of what I did every day.

Sometimes we arrived at a fire too late to make a difference. We threw water on the roof but the house still burned down. Other times we got the job done, protecting lives, whole neighborhoods, and plenty of pets. Those cats and dogs sure chewed me up, but I'm glad I hauled every single one down the ladder.

Most folks have a picture of us loaded with gear rushing into flaming buildings. That's right. This is serious business. But in the quieter moments we also have our share of laughs. We can send a pal flying up into the air with a blast from the pressure hose, and we make our wives crazy planting rusty old hydrants next to the geraniums in our backyards. We have more toy fire trucks than our kids and we get into shouting matches over the best color for emergency vehicles. For the record, I prefer old-fashioned red to that ugly neon yellow.

Above all, we tell stories, the kind where we turn down the TV, kick back in the La-Z-Boy, and relax for a while.

What follows is my favorite. It's about what happened thirteen years ago on the General Edwards drawbridge not far from the redbrick station I call home. It wasn't the first time we had raced there to pry people out of wrecks or scoop up folks who had been hit in the crosswalk.

My first trip to the bridge was back in the Blizzard of '78, when an old man missed the warning light that the ramp was going up. He crashed through the barrier, flew right off the edge, and was submerged in his Pontiac for twenty-nine minutes. We knew because that was how long his Timex had stopped when the divers cut him out from under the ice. He was frozen blue with no pulse, and I went to work breathing life back into him. In a few ticks, his skin turned pink and his eyes blinked open. I was about twenty-four years old, and it was the most amazing thing I'd ever seen.

The *Revere Independent* called it a miracle. I like to think it was God's will. In this line of work, the truth is you try to forget most of your runs, especially the sad ones where people die. If you're lucky they dissolve into a great big blur in your brain. But there are some cases you can never get out of your mind. They stay with you for your whole life. Counting the old man in the ice, I've had three.

When I was just a rookie, I carried a lifeless five-year-old girl from a hellish three-alarm on Squire Road. Her name was Eugenia Louise Cushing, and she was covered in soot. Her pupils were pinpoint, she wasn't breathing, and her blood pressure was undetectable, but I kept trying to revive her. Even when the medical examiner pronounced her dead on the scene and began to fill out the paperwork, I kept going. Then all of a sudden, little Eugenia sat up on the stretcher, coughed, rubbed her eyes, and asked for a glass of milk. That was my first miracle.

I picked up Eugenia's crumpled death certificate and put it away in my wallet. It's all tattered now, but I keep it as reminder that anything is possible in this world.

That brings me to the case of Charlie St. Cloud. Like I said, it starts with a calamity on the drawbridge over the Saugus River, but there's a lot more to it than that. It's about devotion and the unbreakable bond between brothers. It's about finding your soul mate where you least expect. It's about life cut short and love lost. Some folks would call it a tragedy, and I see their point. But I've always tried to find the good in the most desperate situations, and that's why the story of these boys stays with me.

You may think some of this seems far-fetched, even impossible. Believe me, I know we all cling to life and its certainties. It's not easy in these cynical times to cast off the hardness and edge that get us through our days. But try just a little. Open your eyes and you will see what I can see. And if you've ever wondered what happens when a person close to you is taken too soon—and it's always too soon—you may find other truths here, truths that may break the grip of sadness in your life, that may set you free from guilt, that may even bring you back to this world from wherever you are hiding. And then you will never feel alone.

The bulk of this tale takes place here in the snug little village of Marblehead, Massachusetts, a wedge of rock jutting into the Atlantic. It is almost twilight now. I stand in the ancient town cemetery on a sloping hill where two weeping willows and a small mausoleum overlook the harbor. Sailboats tug at moorings, seagulls fly in force, and little boys cast their lines from the dock. Someday they will grow up to hit home runs and kiss girls. Life goes on, infinite, irrepressible.

Nearby, I see a fuzzy old man put a fistful of hollyhocks on his wife's grave. A history buff makes a rubbing from a weathered stone. The tidy rows of monuments drop down to a cove on the water. When I was a school kid, I learned that once upon a time America's first patriots spied from this hilltop on British warships below.

We'll start by going back thirteen years to September 1991. In the rec room at the firehouse, we were polishing off bowls of my wife's famous *spumoni*, arguing about Clarence Thomas, and screaming about the Red Sox, who were chasing the Blue Jays for the pennant. Then we heard the tones on the box, rushed to the rig, and took off.

Now turn the page, come along on the ride, and let me tell you about the death and life of Charlie St. Cloud.

I

RACING
THE MOON

ONE

CHARLIE ST. CLOUD WASN'T THE BEST OR BRIGHTEST BOY in Essex County, but he was surely the most promising. He was junior-class vice president, shortstop of the Marblehead Magicians, and co-captain of the debate club. With a mischievous dimple on one cheek, nose and forehead freckled from the sun, and caramel eyes hidden beneath a flop of sandy-blond hair, he was already handsome at fifteen. He was a friend to jocks and geeks and even had a girlfriend one year older at school. Yes, Charlie St. Cloud was a blessed boy, quick of mind and body, destined for good things, perhaps even a scholarship at Dartmouth, Princeton, or one of those Ivied places.

His mother, Louise, cheered his every achievement. Indeed, Charlie was both cause and cure for her own life's disappointments. Those troubles had begun the very moment he was conceived, an unwanted pregnancy that pushed the man she loved—a carpenter with good hands—right out the door. Next came Charlie's obstructed journey into the world, catching somewhere deep inside and requiring bloody surgery to be born. Soon a second son arrived from another vanished father, and the years blurred into one endless struggle. But for all her woes, Charlie erased her pain with those twinkling eyes and optimism. She had grown to depend on him as her angel, her messenger of hope, and he could do no wrong.

He grew up fast, worked hard at his books, watched out for his mom, and loved his kid brother more than anyone in the world. His name was Sam, and his father—a bail bondsman—was gone, too, barely leaving a trace except for his son's curly brown hair and some bluish bruises on Louise's face. Charlie believed he was the only true protector of his little brother, and someday, together, he knew they would make something of themselves in the world. The boys were three years apart, opposites in coloring and throwing arms, but best friends, united in their love of catching fish, climbing trees, a beagle named Oscar, and the Red Sox.

Then one day, Charlie made a disastrous decision, a mistake the police could not explain and the juvenile court did its best to overlook.

To be precise, Charlie ruined everything on Friday, September 20, 1991.

Mom was working the late shift at Penni's market on Washington Street. The boys had come home from school with mischief on their minds. They had no homework to do until Sunday night. They had already gone spying on the Flynn twins down the block. They had jumped a fence and snuck onto the property of the Czech refugee who claimed to have invented the bazooka. At sunset, they had played catch under the pine trees in their yard on Cloutman's Lane, just as they had done every night since Charlie had given Sam his first Rawlings glove for his seventh birthday. But now it was dark, and they had run out of adventures.

Sam might have settled for crashing and watching Chris Isaak's "Wicked Game" video on MTV, but Charlie had a surprise. He wanted action and had just the plan.

"How 'bout night fishing on Devereux Beach?" he asked Sam, setting his brother up perfectly.

"Boring," Sam said. "We always do that. How 'bout a movie? *Terminator 2*'s playing at the Warwick. Nick Burridge will sneak us in the back."

"I've got a better idea."

"It's R-rated. What's better than that?"

Charlie pulled out two tickets from the pocket of his jeans jacket. Red Sox tickets. They were playing the Yankees. Boston was on a roll, and the evil Bronx Bombers had lost eleven of their last thirteen.

"No way! Where'd those come from?" Sam asked.

"I have my ways."

"How we gonna get there? Fly?"

"Don't you worry about that. Mrs. Pung is on vacation. We can borrow her wagon."

"Borrow? You don't even have a license!"

"You want to go or not?"

"What about Mom?"

"Don't worry. She'll never know."

"We can't leave Oscar. He'll freak out and mess up the house."

"He can come too."

Sure enough, Charlie, Sam, and their beagle were soon driving to Boston in Mrs. Pung's Country Squire. Without their neighbor Mrs. Pung, that is. The police report would make considerable mention of two unlicensed minors, a dog, and a white stolen vehicle with red interior. But Mrs. Pung dropped the auto-theft charges when she got back from Naples, Florida. They were good kids, she said. They only borrowed the car. They made a terrible mistake. They more than paid the price.

The drive took thirty minutes, and Charlie was especially careful on Route 1A where the Swampscott and Lynn cops patrolled. The boys listened to the pregame show on WRKO, talked about the last time they'd been to the ballpark, and counted their money, calculating they had enough for two Fenway Franks each, a Coke, and peanuts.

"This is our year," Sam said. "The Sox'll win the Series."

"They just have to break the Curse of the Bambino," Charlie said. It was the superstition of every red-blooded Boston fan: Trading Babe Ruth to the Yankees had put a hex on the Sox.

"You don't believe in that stuff, do you?"

"Think about it. The Sox haven't won the Series since 1918. The Yanks have done it twenty-two times. You do the math."

"C'mon, the Babe didn't make Bill Buckner boot that ground ball in '86." Buckner was the reviled first baseman who let an easy dribbler through his legs in the World Series, costing the Sox game six and, many swore, the championship.

"How do you know?"

"He just didn't."

"Well, I think he did."

"Did not."

"Did too."

A standoff.

"Draw?" Sam said reluctantly.

"Okay, draw."

And with that, the argument was done but not over. A draw was their way of stopping a dispute that would have gone on all night. It would be dutifully recorded in *Charlie & Sam's Book of Big & Small Arguments*. And after the proper procedural motions, it could be started up again at any point. Ignoring their age difference, Sam threw himself into these arguments with passion, and the two brothers often spent hours in the Abbot public library on Pleasant Street gathering ammunition for their battles.

Now, with its red bricks and shimmering glass, Boston was waiting across the Charles River. They turned down Brookline Avenue and could see the hazy lights of the stadium. Biting at the chilly air, Oscar leaned out the window. With his red and white coat, he was the perfect mascot for the adventure.

In the parking lot, the boys stuffed their beagle into a backpack and took off for the bleachers. As they reached their seats a thundering cheer rose for Roger Clemens, #21, throwing his first rocket. The boys laughingly bowed left and right to acknowledge the crowd. A stadium guard would later testify he saw the two unaccompanied youths, wearing caps and carrying mitts, but did not stop or question them.

Their seats were in right field, directly behind a guy who must have been seven feet tall, but it didn't matter. It could have poured, it could have snowed. Nothing could ruin the spectacle of the Green Monster in left field, the grass, the chalk lines, and the infield dirt. They were right near Pesky's pole, just 302 feet from home plate, easy distance for catching a home run.

One of their heroes, Wade Boggs, sat out the game with a sore right shoulder, but Jody Reed took his place and delivered, with a run-scoring double and homer off the left-field foul pole. The boys ate two hot dogs each with extra relish. Oscar got some Cracker Jacks from a woman in the next row. A big bearded guy next to her gave them a few sips of Budweiser. Charlie was careful not to drink too much. Still, the police report would mention traces of alcohol in their blood. There was enough to raise questions, but not enough for answers.

Clemens shut out the Yankees, allowing only three hits and striking out seven. The crowd cheered, and Oscar howled. With the final out and a 2–0 victory in the books, the fans scattered but the boys stayed in their seats, replaying the highlights. The team was now miraculously within striking distance of Toronto. Instead of falling apart in September, always the cruelest month, the Sox were surging.

"Someday, we'll have season tickets," Charlie said. "Right there behind home plate in the first row."

"The bleachers are good enough for me," Sam said, eating the last of the peanuts. "I don't care about the seats. As long as it's you and me, that's what makes baseball great."

"We'll always play ball, Sam. No matter what."

The stadium lights began shutting down. The ground crew had just about spread the tarp over the infield.

"We better go," Charlie said.

The boys headed for the parking lot, where the white station wagon was all alone. The drive home was much faster. Springsteen was born to run on the radio. There was hardly any traffic. The trip would take half an hour. They would be home by 10:30. Mom wouldn't be back until midnight. Mrs. Pung in Florida would never know.

Just past the Wonderland Greyhound Park, Sam pulled a cassette from his pocket and stuck it in the radio. It was U2's *The Joshua Tree*. Charlie sang along to "With or Without You."

"Bono rocks," Sam said.

"The Boss."

"Bono."

"The Boss."

"Draw?"

"Draw."

They drove silently for a while, then Sam asked out of the blue, "How long will it be until I'm grown up?"

"You already are," Charlie answered.

"I'm serious. When do I stop being a kid?"

"Officially," Charlie said, "when you're twelve, you're a man and you can do what you want."

"Says who?"

"Says me."

"I'm a man and I can do what I want," Sam said, enjoying the sound of it. A great moon floated on the Saugus River, and he rolled down the window. "Look," he said. "It's bigger tonight. Must be closer to us."

"Nah," Charlie said. "It's always the same distance. That's just an optical illusion."

"What's that?"

"When your eye plays tricks on you."

"What kind of trick?"

"Wherever it is in the sky," Charlie said, "it's always 225,745 miles away." He did the math. Numbers were easy for him. "At our speed right now, it would take about 170 days to get there."

"Mom wouldn't be too crazy about that," Sam said.

"And Mrs. Pung wouldn't be happy about the mileage."

The boys laughed. Then Sam said, "It's no optical delusion. It's closer tonight. I swear. Look, you can see a halo just like an angel's."

"No such thing," Charlie said. "That's a refraction of the ice crystals in the upper atmosphere."

"Gee, I thought it was a refraction of the ice crystals on your butt!" Sam howled with laughter, and Oscar barked in a series of sharp, distinctive woofs.

Charlie checked his mirrors, aimed the car straight ahead, and took one quick glance to the right. The moon was flickering between the iron railings of the drawbridge, keeping pace with them as they sped home. It sure seemed closer than ever tonight. He turned his head for a better look. He thought the bridge was empty so he pushed down on the gas.

Of all his reckless decisions that night, surely this was the worst. Charlie raced the moon, and in the final second before the end, he saw the perfect image of happiness. Sam's innocent face looking up at him. The curl dangling over his forehead. The Rawlings glove on his hand. And then there was only fracturing glass, metal, and blackness.

TWO

WITH A COLD WIND RUSHING THROUGH THE SPANS IN THE
General Edwards bridge, Florio Ferrente snatched the
jaws of life from the back of his rig. The serrated
blades weighed forty-one pounds and could chop
through steel, but he wielded them like kitchen scis-
sors in his hulking hands.

Florio kneeled for a moment and offered the fireman's prayer that came to his lips every time he went
to work.

Give me courage.

Give me strength.

Please, Lord, through it all, be at my side.

Then came the blur of action. One thousand—one
million—calculations and considerations. All instanta-
neous. He evaluated the spilled gasoline and the
chance of a spark or explosion. He assessed the fastest

way into the wreck—through the windshield, hood, or doors? And he did the math on how much time he had for this rescue. Time, precious time.

Florio ran past the jagged skid marks and jackknifed tractor trailer. He didn't bother to stop for the truck driver leaning against the center divider. The man's head was in his hands. He reeked of beer and blood. It was one of the rules of rescue: Heaven protects fools and drunks. The guy would be fine.

The instant license-plate check on the white wagon had produced the first bit of information. The Ford belonged to Mrs. Norman Pung of Cloutman's Lane, Marblehead. Age: 73. Vision-impaired. Perhaps the first clue.

The vehicle was crunched and tossed upside down, like a cockroach, its front end smashed into the railing of the bridge. He could tell from the trail of glass and metal that the car had rolled at least twice. Florio dropped to the pavement and peered through a squashed window.

There was no noise inside. No sound of breathing or moaning. Blood trickled through cracks in the metal.

With swift movements, he jammed a power spreader into the narrow space between the hood and door. A quick flick of his thumb and the hydraulics surged. The car frame groaned as the machine drove the metal apart, clearing a narrow crawl space. Florio pushed his head inside the wreck and saw two boys, upside down, unconscious, tangled in seat belts. Their twisted arms were wrapped around each other in a bloody embrace. No sign of Mrs. Pung.

"Two traumatic arrests up front," he shouted to his partner, Trish Harrington. "A dog in back. Scoop and run. Priority One."

He slid out of the wreckage and shoved the Hurst tool into the hinges of the door. Another jab of the thumb, and the blades took two powerful bites. Florio pulled the door right off and threw it across the pavement.

"Gimme two C-spine collars," he yelled. "And two short backboards."

He crawled back inside. "Can you hear me?" he said to the smaller boy. "Talk to me." No response. No movement. The kid's face and neck were wet with blood, eyes and lips swollen.

It was another rule of rescue: If the child is quiet, be scared.

Florio wrapped a brace around the boy's neck, strapped on a backboard, then cut the seat belt with his knife. He lowered the patient gently and pulled him out onto the pavement. He was slight, around eighty pounds, and, incredibly, was still wearing a Rawlings baseball glove on one hand.

"Pupils are blown," Florio said, checking with his flashlight. "He's posturing. Blood from the ears." Bad signs, all. Time to go after the other victim. He climbed back inside. The teenager was pinned beneath the steering column. Florio wedged another spreader into the foot space and hit the hydraulics. As the metal separated, he could see one open fracture of the femur. And he smelled the awful brew of radiator fluid and blood.

He collared the boy quickly and tied the back brace into place, then pulled him out and carefully set him down on the pavement.

"Can you hear me?" he said. Not a word.

"Squeeze my hand if you can hear me," he said. Nothing.

The two young victims were now lying side by side on backboards. The little dog in the backseat was hopeless, crushed between the rear axle and the trunk. What a waste. "St. Francis," he whispered, "bless this creature with your grace."

Florio checked his watch. This was the golden hour: less than sixty minutes to save their lives. If he could stabilize them and get them to the trauma surgeons, they might survive.

He and his partner lifted the first boy into their ambulance. Then the second. Trish ran around to the driver's seat. Florio climbed in back and leaned out to pull the doors shut. On the horizon, he saw the full moon. God dropped it there, he was sure, as a reminder of our small place in the world. A reminder that what is beautiful is fleeting.

Then the ambulance lurched forward, and the siren screamed. He pulled the doors closed. For an instant, his fingers found the well-worn gold medallion around his neck. It was St. Jude of Desperate Situations.

Show me the way . . .

He put his stethoscope to the chest of the younger boy. He listened and knew the simple truth.

This was a time for miracles.

THREE

A MIST SHROUDED THE GROUND, MUFFLING THE SOUNDS of the world. Charlie, Sam, and Oscar huddled in the damp and dark. There was no one else around. They could have been anywhere or nowhere. It didn't matter. They were together.

"Mom will kill us for this," Sam said, shivering. He smacked his fist into his mitt. "She's gonna be mad. Really mad."

"Don't worry, little man," Charlie said. He pushed the curls from his brother's face. "I'll take care of it."

He could imagine his mother's disappointment: her forehead turning red, the veins in her temples pulsing, her devastating frown with those little lines scrunching around her lips.

"They'll send us to jail for this," Sam said. "Mrs. Pung will make us pay, and we don't have any money."

He turned his head and focused on a jagged shape in the murk. There it was—the carcass of the station wagon. What hadn't been destroyed in the crash had been cut to pieces by the rescuers.

"You won't go to jail," Charlie said. "You're not old enough. They wouldn't punish a twelve-year-old that way. Maybe me, I was driving; but not you."

"What are we gonna do?" Sam said.

"I'll think of something."

"I'm sorry," Sam said. "It was my fault."

"No, it wasn't."

"I distracted you with the moon."

"No, you didn't. I should've seen the truck and gotten out of the way."

Sam thwacked his glove. The sound fell flat in the nothingness. Another thwack. "So now what?" he said.

"Give me a minute," Charlie said. "I'm thinking." He looked around, trying to make sense of the landscape. There was no sign of the bridge, no curve of the river, no outline of the city. The sky was a blanket of black. He searched for Polaris, the North Star. He scanned for any constellation to give him bearings. All he could see were shapes moving in the distance, solids in the fluid of night.

And then through the gloom, he began to realize where they were. Somehow, mysteriously, they had been transported to a small hill with two drooping willows overlooking the harbor. He recognized the curve of the shore with its huddle of masts bobbing on the water and the green glow of the lighthouse.

"I think we're home," he said.

"How'd that happen?"

"No idea, but look, there's Tucker's wharf."

He pointed, but Sam wasn't interested. "Mom's going to ground us," Sam said. "We better make up a good story, or she'll use the belt."

"No, she won't," Charlie said. "I'm coming up with a plan right now. Trust me."

But he had no idea what to do or how to get them out of this jam. Then he saw another light in the distance, faint at first, but growing brighter. Maybe a flashlight or a rescue party. Oscar began to bark, friendly at first, then he let out a long yowl.

"Look," Sam said. "Who's that?"

"Oh shit." Charlie never swore, and Sam tensed up.

"Is that Mom?"

"No, I don't think so."

"Then who? Who's coming? I'm scared."

The light was warm and bright, and it was getting closer.

"Don't be afraid," Charlie said.

They were dead and gone.

No pulse. No breath. Hypoxic. No oxygen in the blood, from cardiac arrest brought on by blunt trauma. Dead and gone. Florio flashed his light stick one more time into the blown pupils of the older boy. They were black and bottomless.

He stuck leads on the kid's wrists and left chest, then punched the button on the monitor. The line on the six-second ECG strip was flat.

"This is Medic Two," he said into the radio. "I've got two crunch cases. Pulseless nonbreathers."

Florio grabbed his intubation kit and slipped the curved steel blade of the laryngoscope into the boy's mouth. Pushing aside the kid's slack tongue, he aimed for the entryway to the trachea, a small gap between the vocal cords. He pressed harder and the instrument eased into position. Perfect. With a whirl of motion, he inflated the cuff, fastened the ambu bag, and began to ventilate.

The vehicle hurtled toward the North Shore ER, and Florio knew there was really only one chance left. So he pulled out the Zoll defibrillator paddles, pressed them to the kid's bare chest, pushed the button with his thumb, and blasted him with 250 joules.

Damn.

The monitor showed no cardiac conversion. The heart was still in V-fib, quivering like Jell-O in a bowl. In rapid mechanical movements, Florio clamped a tourniquet on the kid's arm, found a vein, jabbed a needle, plugged in an IV line, and pumped epinephrine. Then he dialed up 300 joules.

He pressed the button, and the body convulsed. Again no luck, but Florio had been here before. He had saved countless diabetics in hypoglycemic seizure with shots of D50. He had rescued dozens of heroin OD's with blasts of Narcan. He never gave up. It was never too late for miracles. Even when a casket was covered with dirt, it wasn't necessarily over. Over the years, he had collected clippings about the dead rising up and banging on their coffins to get out. He was especially fond of the case in South Africa of the reverend who stunned mourners at his own funeral when he joined in the chorus of his favorite hymn from inside the casket. And there was the Greek Orthodox bishop lying in state as congregants paid their final respects. When church bells began to ring, he woke up, climbed down from the catafalque, and demanded to know why everyone was staring.

So Florio dialed up 320 joules on the Zoll and hit the button. The body in front of him heaved from the shock. This was the last chance. Unless he could get the boy back into regular cardiac rhythm, it was over.

FOUR

THE GLOOM WAS GONE, AND THE LIGHT HAD ALMOST
encircled them.

Sam was shaking now and had wrapped his arms
around Oscar. "I'm afraid," he said. "I don't want to
get in trouble. I don't want Mom to yell. I don't want
strangers to take us away."

"It's gonna be okay," Charlie said. "Trust me." He
felt the warmth of the light reach all the way inside,
and the pain began to go away.

"Promise you won't leave me," Sam said, reaching
for his hand.

"Promise."

"Swear?"

"Swear."

"Cross your heart and hope to die?"

"Yeah," Charlie said. "Now promise you won't leave me either."

"Never," Sam said. His eyes were wide and clear. His face was tranquil. He had never looked so peaceful before.

They hugged each other, then stood side by side, feeling the light come over them, a brilliant blur of white and gold.

"Don't worry, little man," Charlie said once more. "Everything'll be okay. I promise."

Florio heard the monitor beep.

Perhaps it was St. Florian. Or St. Jude. Or simply God's grace. He pulled the paddles from the boy's chest and saw the burn marks on his skin. The ECG strip showed the boy's heart had suddenly flipped back into a regular beat. Then, incredibly, his eyes opened slowly. They were the color of caramel and surrounded by exploded capillaries. He coughed and stared straight up. His was the abstract look of having traveled a great distance.

"Welcome back," Florio said.

The boy seemed confused and worried, both perfectly normal under the circumstances.

"Where's Sam?" he muttered. "I was just talking to Sam. I promised—"

"What's your name?"

"—I promised Sam I wouldn't leave him."

"Tell me your name, son."

"St. Cloud," he said faintly. "Charlie St. Cloud."

"You're gonna be okay, St. Cloud. I'm doing the best I can for Sam." Florio crossed himself and prayed silently.

Thank You for the gift of breath.
For the gift of life.
For the gift of every moment . . .
Then he heard Charlie say again, "Where's Sam? Where's my brother? I can't leave him. . . ."

The words didn't really make much sense, but Charlie understood the urgency in the man's voice. It was a tenseness that adults always showed when things weren't going well. When they were out of control. The paramedic was working on Sam right beside him.

Systolic pressure is 60.
He's no longer posturing.
Unable to intubate.
Then Charlie felt a wave of pain in his back and neck. He grimaced and cried out.

"I'm here with you," the paramedic said. "I'm giving you something that'll make you sleepy. Don't worry."

Charlie felt warmth spreading through his shoulders, down his legs. Everything grew blurry, but he knew one thing for sure. He had given his word to his little brother. A promise to take care of him. Their fathers may have come and gone, but no matter what happened, he would never leave Sam.

Sure, they would be in giant trouble. Mom would ground them for a long, long time. But nothing was ever permanent. No matter what she did, there was no stopping them from growing up. No stopping them at all.

In Charlie's numbed mind, a parade of images floated along:

Someday soon, they'd be old enough to leave home, go to college, get real jobs, and live near each other. They'd have families. They'd play catch with their own boys and have season tickets to the Sox.

Charlie had never really imagined the future before. He lived in the present tense with Sam and Oscar. But in that moment, his neck in a brace, an IV in his arm, he somehow pictured the days and years ahead—the days and years with his brother at his side, always together, no matter what. There was no alternative. Life without Sam was simply unfathomable.

He reached out across the narrow divide of the ambulance. He pushed his hand past the thick waist of a paramedic. He found Sam's skinny arm, the IV, the baseball mitt wedged next to his body. He felt his brother's hand, all limp and cold. And Charlie held on as hard as he could.

II

DIVE FOR
DREAMS

FIVE

THE FLAGS ON THE WHARF WHIPPED IN UNISON AS TESS
Carroll pulled her banged-up '74 Chevy Cheyenne to a
stop. She got out of the truck and studied the snapping
shapes in the wind. There were tiny clues in every
curl, subtle hints in each twist. She knew this was a
calming southeasterly breeze, no more than four
knots. It began up in the ice floes of Nova Scotia, blew
down with the trades over New England, and eventually would meander all the way to the Caribbean.

Tess walked to the flatbed and tried to open the
tailgate but the darn thing wouldn't budge. She had
bought the old pickup from a junkyard, and her dad
had put life into it with a used engine. When it needed
another motor, he told her to trade it in. She didn't listen, and years later when he died without warning,
she knew she would never get rid of that Chevy. She

kept it running herself now, holding on to the smooth steering wheel like it was a piece of him.

Tess reached over the siding, grabbed hold of a big nylon sail bag, and hauled it out. She was tall and lean with dark straight hair in a ponytail that poked through the back of a Patriots' cap. She balanced the sack on one shoulder, turned, and walked toward the dock.

Bella Hooper was sitting in the sun on an aluminum lawn chair with a hand-painted sign propped next to her advertising: THE WOMAN WHO LISTENS. When she saw Tess coming, she lifted up one Walkman earphone and bellowed, "Pull up a seat!" A bartender for thirty years at Maddie's, Bella had retired a few years back to start a new business. For $15 an hour, she would listen to anything you had to say, confidentiality guaranteed. She didn't dispense advice, and she definitely didn't accept health insurance, but she was always busy with clients who came down to the dock to give her an earful. Bella's great gift—perhaps even art—was the ability to keep a one-way conversation aloft with just the proper number of "uh-huhs" and "oohs" and "then whats."

"C'mon, Tess, I'll give you my special friends-and-family discount," she was saying. "Only five bucks for an hour of quality listening."

"Too bad you don't take Blue Cross," Tess said with a smile. "Maybe next time. I've got to get out on the water."

"Suit yourself," Bella said, adjusting her earphones and settling back into her lawn chair.

Up ahead, a few old wharf rats were playing pinochle on a bench. They were retired fishermen who got by on Social

Security and keno jackpots and who lounged around by the water every afternoon, keeping track of boats, monitoring the price of lobster, and telling lies.

"Hey, princess!" an old-timer rasped, peering through Larry King glasses that dominated his scraggly face.

"How you doing, Bony?" Tess said.

"Losing my shirt," he said, throwing down his cards. "Need a crew for the afternoon?"

"Wish I could afford you."

"I'm begging," he said. "I'll work for free. I can't take another minute here."

"He can't take another losing hand," one of the guys cracked.

"Please, Tess, let me sail with you."

"You really want another heart attack?" Tess said, adjusting the sail bag. "You know I'll give you one." She winked.

"Whip!" Bony said, using the local slang for "damn" that had been passed down for generations.

"Down bucket!" Tess answered. For reasons lost to time, it was the automatic response, a phrase that had been coined when slops were thrown out of windows in centuries past. Marblehead was indeed an ancient and cloistered place, where only fourth-generation residents earned the right to call themselves true "Headers." Everyone else was considered a new arrival, and townies used expressions like "whip" to separate themselves from the off-islanders who had invaded the peninsula, pushed up prices, and brought cappuccino to Pleasant Street.

"See ya later," Tess said, heading down the dock.

"Watch out for the weather," Bony called out.

"Will do, and try not to break any hearts while I'm gone."

The gang laughed as she walked on. She was wearing khakis with flowery patches on both knees, a white tank top, and an oversize blue button-down. Her eyes were a soft shade of green, and her nose came to an impossibly fine point, the kind women in Los Angeles and New York paid plastic surgeons thousands to create. She was one of those lucky New Englanders who always looked great at yacht-club clambakes or at the ice rink for midnight broomball. Indeed, she was a natural beauty who never bothered with the mirror except to make sure she wasn't bloody after a rough night at the mast.

Tess strolled along the dock toward her gleaming thirty-eight-foot sloop, an Aerodyne with a slate-blue hull, an immaculate white deck, and QUERENCIA painted in gold on the stern. The tide was half and rising, and she could smell the seaweed and salt in the air.

"You going to help or just sit there?" she said to a massive mound of a man who was dangling his feet over the side of the yacht.

"You're doing fine without me," Tink Wetherbee said, standing up and straightening his T-shirt that announced in bold letters: MAY BE USED AS A FLOTATION DEVICE. He was 6'4", with a chest as puffed out as a spinnaker, a furry face, and shaggy brown hair that he chopped himself. Tess liked to joke that if Tink strapped a barrel around his neck, he would look exactly like a St. Bernard.

"You know," he was saying as she stepped aboard with the sail bag balanced on her shoulder, "you're pretty strong for a girl."

"You mean, pretty strong for a girl who signs your paycheck and could kick your sorry ass," Tess said, heaving the sack toward him. It hit squarely in his prodigious stomach, and he stumbled back.

"What's sorry about my ass?" He held on to the sail bag and craned his neck for a look.

"Trust me, Tink. It's a sorry sight." Tess hopped into the cockpit of the boat, elbowing him in the ribs as she went by. "Just one more week," she said as she untied the wheel. "One more week and I'm gone. Think you'll miss me?"

"Miss you? Did the slaves miss their masters?"

"Funny," she said, taking the covers off the navigation instruments. "So how's our mainsail? Ready for the big trip?"

"The best we've ever built," he said. "You'll be the envy of the world."

"I like the way that sounds." She stretched her arms and back, reaching first to the sky, then down to her red Converse high-tops. Her body ached from all the preparations of the past few months. She had done thousands of military presses and biceps curls. She had run and swum hundreds of miles. Every step and stroke had been carefully calculated so she would be ready to lash sails in Force 10 winds, stand long watches in high seas, and haul anchors.

Next week with the blast of the starting cannon, Tess would set sail on a solo race around the world and, if lucky, ride the wind more than 30,000 miles. It was the greatest adventure in sports—the dream of a lifetime—and an enormous opportunity for her sail-making business. Fewer people had circumnavigated the world alone than had climbed Mt. Everest, and Tess's goal was to become one of the first ten women ever to make the journey. So far only eight had succeeded.

The whole community was rooting for her, holding bake sales and lobster cookouts to raise money for the quest, and the select-men even passed an official resolution declaring her an ambassador to the world. Starting in Boston Harbor, the race itself would be covered by every TV station in New England, and journalists around the globe would track her progress. Even the town teenagers were onboard—Mrs. Paternina's science class at the high school promised to e-mail every day with news from home.

Tink kneeled on the deck and pulled the mainsail from the canvas bag. The sheet was folded like an accordion, and he began to spread it out. Tess bent down to help. "It's gorgeous," she said, stroking the green taffeta outer layer. This wasn't any old piece of sailcloth, like the one she had cut from a bedsheet and stitched for her first boat. This main was a state-of-the-art laminate with Kevlar fibers, built to ride out the worst weather in the world, and everyone in her company had worked weeks fine-tuning it.

"Sure hope we spelled my name right," she said, pulling the corner of the sail to the mast, where she unscrewed a shackle and attached the tack. She kneeled on the deck, turned the winch, and began feeding sail to Tink. Inch by inch, he put the slides on their track, and the green sheet began to climb the mast.

Tess smiled as the triangle emblazoned with her company name—CARROLL SAILS—took to the sky. Mariners on five continents would see it, and with any luck, they would want one for their own.

She turned the winch more slowly now, and the main was almost two-thirds up the mast. Almost unconsciously, she felt light air tousle her hair. Without checking the weather vane, she knew the wind was from the northeast, the first feelers of that low pressure. The susurrus of the sails, luffed by the breeze, and the tickle on the back of her neck told her it would be rough later on the water.

Tess loved the wind and its ways. As a girl, it had been her constant companion. From a sunny morning twenty years ago when she ventured into the harbor in her first Brutal Beast, she had always tracked the ripples on the water and the lean of the tall grass on the shore. She knew the difference between true and apparent wind, and she had mastered the air in every form, flying hang gliders and sailplanes, racing Windsurfers and catamarans, and—to the horror of her mother—thrilling to the free-fall of parachutes.

As a woman, she had made the wind her livelihood. Straight out of Williams with a physics degree, she went to work for Hood Sails in Newport, learning fast and immersing herself in the advanced science of modern sail design. She worshiped Ted Hood, a Marbleheader and America's Cup skipper, who knew more about striking a curve on a spinnaker than anyone on earth. But after a couple of years, she realized she just didn't like having a boss, and even worse, she hated spending her days running computer models on lift and drag ratios. So with $186.40 in the bank, she quit and moved home.

Dad went in on a bank loan with her, and she opened her own sail loft on Front Street, determined to compete with the big boys. Within a year, she had hired a dozen of the smartest designers, cutters, and sewers in the area. She made a family of them, paid them better than anyone around, and encouraged this team to dream up ways to make boats go faster.

Now the wind was picking up, and Tess cranked the winch,

but the sail suddenly seemed to jam. She pushed hard on the handle, then Tink gave a hand, but the sail wouldn't move.

"Better get up there to take a look," she said.

"Want to hoist me?" he said, patting his belly.

"Nobody's that strong." She walked over to one of the lockers, pulled out the bowswain's chair, fastened it to another halyard, and positioned herself on the wooden seat.

"Up, up, and away," she said, and with a few good tugs of the line, Tink lifted her in the air.

A seagull wheeled overhead as Tess soared to the top of the forty-seven-foot mast. She grabbed hold of the pole and could tell immediately that the halyard was jammed.

"Release the downhaul," she yelled to Tink. Then she reached into her pocket for her army knife, jammed the point under the halyard, and lifted it back into the sheave.

"We're clear," she shouted. "Just give me one more second. I love it up here." She looked down on the town curving along the waterfront. She saw fishermen on the rocks casting for stripers. Across the harbor, kids were flying kites on Riverhead Beach. In the distance, she made out the mausoleums and obelisks of Waterside Cemetery sloping down to the shore. Her dad was buried there under a Japanese maple. When her mother chose the spot, she wanted him to have a perfect view of the harbor.

Marblehead was definitely her favorite place on earth, a world unto itself. Sure, there were 20,377 people living on the peninsula, but it felt like a small town. Most folks had spent their whole lives here and never even thought about leaving. They were born at Mary Alley Hospital. They were raised on blueberry pancakes at the Driftwood and Joe Frogger cookies at the Rusty Rudder.

They went to movies at the Warwick and got drunk at Maddie's. They gathered at the Landing every December to watch Santa and Mrs. Claus arrive by lobster boat for the Christmas Walk. They married at the Old North Church and celebrated at the Gerry function hall. And in the end, when they sailed over to the other side, they were buried in Waterside.

But, much as she loved Marblehead, Tess believed there was more for her out there beyond the rocks. There was a world to see and, God willing, great love to find. Over the years, she had given a good look at every eligible guy in town, all seven of them. She had dated fellows from Boston to Burlington. But after a series of misses across New England, she knew she wasn't going to find her Prince Charming or even a Regular Joe who would know what to make of her. So she was determined to venture beyond. Somewhere in Australia or New Zealand, she dreamed of meeting a dashing millionaire who spoke three languages, restored fifty-seven-foot classic boats, and was tall enough to twirl her around in her heels.

Her sea journey would take four months, maybe more, and to be honest, there were no guarantees she would ever make it back. Her mother seemed to know every case of a solo sailor vanishing or skirting death, like the Canadian who sank off the Canary Islands, escaped in a life raft with three pounds of food and eight pints of water, and survived seventy-six days.

"Hey, girl, you're not getting any lighter up there," Tink shouted from below.

"Sorry," she said. "Just trying to memorize what everything looks like."

Back on deck and out of the harness, Tess made for the cockpit, where she pulled out a clipboard with her checklist. This weekend trip was her last chance to make sure everything—absolutely everything—was shipshape. She would inspect the sails, autopilots, electronics, and survival equipment. Then she would take a few days off with her family and friends, and try to relax before the starting gun next week.

She could feel Tink's breath as he peered over her shoulder at the list.

"You sure you don't want me to come along?" Tink said. "You know, in case it gets lonely or cold out there." He nudged her with a big paw.

"Nice offer, but I don't need any more ballast onboard."

"Who's going to hoist you when the main gets stuck again?"

"I'll figure something out," Tess said. "Now tell me about that low-pressure front. What's the deal?"

"It's not good," he said, pulling a computer printout from his pocket and unfolding it. In the sail loft, Tink was in charge of cutting and sewing. For the big trip, he was Tess's go-to guy and meteorologist. He had worked in Bangor as one of those jovial TV weathermen doling out forecasts and cheer, but his broadcasting career ended prematurely. One night on the eleven o'clock news, he got fed up with a blow-dried, emaciated anchorwoman and called her a "skeletal gasbag." No one disputed the characterization, not even the station manager, but Tink lost his job anyway. So he threw out his hairspray and makeup, moved to the North Shore, and went into sail-making and marine forecasting.

"It looks like a lot of low pressure coming down from Maine," he was saying. "You can see the isobars on the back side of the depression."

"That means more wind," Tess said, grinning.

"Wish you weren't going out at all, but you better head south-west and get ahead of the storm. Don't want you to break any-thing on this boat before you have to."

"See you Sunday, big guy."

"Radio if you need me," he said, going to the rail. "And re-member, I'll be pining away for you."

"Pining away with a few hot dogs at tonight's game?"

"I'll have an extra one for you." Tink jumped down to the dock as Tess turned the key, and the onboard engine rumbled. She put one fist on the throttle and was ready to push off when she heard a voice call out.

"Hey, sailor," a woman said from the wharf. She was in her late fifties, with fluffs of gray hair poking over a sun visor. "Got a good-bye kiss for an old lady?"

Grace Carroll was every inch as tall as her daughter, and de-spite hip-replacement surgery a few years ago, she moved up the gangway with forceful steps. "I was in the kitchen looking out the window and I saw you on the mast," she said. "Thought I'd come down to say hi."

"Awww, Mom," Tess said, "I'm sorry I didn't call. I've been so busy—"

"Don't worry about me," Grace said, stepping aboard. "I've been running around like crazy getting the fund-raiser ready for next week." For years, Grace had been on the board of the Female Humane Society, the town's oldest charity, which was founded after a gale turned seventy-five Marblehead women into widows in the early 1800s. "Just be careful out there," she was saying. "I'm counting on you to entertain all the old ladies."

"I'll be there," Tess said. "Don't worry."

"Don't forget WBZ is coming Wednesday to interview me about your race. Better tell me what to say or I may embarrass you." She chuckled, looked up and down *Querencia*, then said, "Dad would be so proud, and darn jealous too."

It was true. He would be proud *and* jealous. He had taught her to tack in a little tub with a broomstick mast. He had cheered when at age five she won her first race week series in a Turnabout. Above all, he had encouraged her to live boldly and see how far she could go in the world. "Dive for dreams," he used to say, quoting the e. e. cummings poem. "And live by love."

When the heart attack hit him two years ago—no doubt from too many lobster rolls at Kelly's in Revere—a gaping hole opened up in Tess's universe. She had tried everything to fill the void, but it was futile. So she decided to do what he told her—push the limits and see how far she could go. Her race around the world was in honor of him.

"When will you be back?" Grace said.

"Sunday for dinner, or maybe sooner. Depends on the wind."

"Want me to make chowder?"

"More than anything in the world."

Grace ran her hand through her hair, then said, "Tell me something. Who on earth am I going to feed every Sunday night when you're gone?"

"That's easy," Tess said. "Tink and Bobo."

"Bobo? That old hound. He'll eat me out of house and home! You sure you can't bring him around the world?"

"Wish I could, but it's against the regs. No companions allowed."

"Silly rules. What's the point without a companion?" Grace's pale eyes managed somehow to ask questions without words, and Tess knew exactly what her mother was wondering: Why haven't you found one yet? Why haven't you settled down? Why haven't you said yes to either of those two marriage proposals? Then, Grace's expression changed, and she was back in the moment. "Love you," she said. "Have a good sail. And don't forget you need to go see Nana when you get back. She could use a hug from her granddaughter." She turned to go back down the gangway, but Tess stopped her with a hand on the shoulder.

"Come here, Mom," she said, opening her arms. She pulled her tight, the way Dad always did, and thought for a moment her mother might break in her arms. It was as if Grace's body had shrunk from the lack of physical contact and the absence of her life companion. Tess could feel her mom's arms around her, too, squeezing, as if she didn't want to let go.

After a few moments, they released each other. Grace pinched Tess's cheek, kissed her, and walked down to the dock.

Tess leaned forward on the throttle. The boat glided away from the slip, moved into the channel, and passed a thousand vessels moored in the harbor. She inspected the clipboard with the weather map and the course Tink had charted. A thick black line zigzagged southeast past Halfway Rock, then west through the Cape Cod Canal into Buzzard's Bay, then angled back. It was the easy route, away from the low pressure bearing down from the north.

But Tess wanted action. She wanted to tense the sails and feel the speed. She could hear the boat creaking, anxious to get going. The sheets flapped against the mast. On the horizon, she could see a vast expanse of gray altocumulus clouds with small ridges underneath like fish scales. She thought of the mariner's rhyme, "Mare's tails and mackerel scales make tall ships carry low sails." It would be blowing hard in a few hours, just the way she liked it.

When she cleared the harbor mouth and passed the light, she aimed the boat on an unlikely course. Her compass indicated a 58-degree heading straight for the Eagle Island Channel and the Powers Rock buoy. For Tess, the easy route was never an option. If she couldn't make it through a little low pressure, how would she ever get all the way around the world? So she eased the sheet to a broad reach and filled the mainsail with wind. Then she watched her instrument dials leap as *Querencia* gained speed and rode a rising wind straight into the storm.

SIX

THE WOMAN IN THE BLACK DRESS WEPT.

She kneeled beside a gravestone and clutched the granite slab with one hand. Her frail body jerked with every sob, and her gray hair, wrapped in a careful bun, seemed to shake loose strand by strand.

Charlie St. Cloud watched from behind a boxwood hedge. He recognized the woman but kept his distance. He was respectful of the pain. There would be a time to step forward and offer a helping hand, but not now. So he tucked his work gloves in his back pocket, unwrapped a piece of Bazooka, tossed it in his mouth, and waited.

He had opened this very grave that morning, carried the casket from the hearse, lowered it into the ground, and backfilled the job when the funeral was done. It was the only burial of the day in Waterside

Cemetery. Work was pretty quiet. One of Charlie's men was out trimming hedges. Another was pressure-washing monuments. A third was collecting branches that had come down in a storm. September was always the slowest month of the year in the funeral business. Charlie wasn't sure exactly why, but he knew December and January were definitely the busiest. Folks passed away more often in the coldest months, and he wondered if it was the frost or a natural response to the excess of the holidays.

Thirteen years had gone by since Charlie had first come to Waterside. Thirteen years had passed since the paramedics failed to revive his little brother. Thirteen years had vanished since Sam was buried in a small coffin near the Forest of Shadows. Thirteen Octobers. Thirteen World Series. Thirteen years keeping the promise.

Charlie was still a handsome young man with a flop of sandy hair. That mischievous dimple in one cheek always flashed when he smiled, and his caramel eyes melted just about everyone he met. With each passing year, his mother insisted he looked more like his father—a compliment of sorts because the only picture he had ever seen of his dad showed a rugged man on a motorcycle with shiny aviator sunglasses propped on his head.

Charlie had grown a few more inches and stood 6'3". His shoulders were square and his arms well muscled from hauling caskets and stone. The only legacy of the accident was a slight limp, and it was barely noticeable. The doctors had said the pins, screws, and plates in his femur and fibula would set off metal detectors—but he never had the chance to find out.

After the crash, he had finished high school, spent a couple of years at Salem State College, and gotten a degree in emergency medicine. He was a licensed paramedic, but no matter how hard he tried to move away, he could never go too far from Waterside. Even the love of a pretty teacher in Peabody couldn't pull him away, for he was always drawn back to this place and the promise.

Waterside was his world, eighty acres of grass and granite encircled by wrought iron. He lived in the caretaker's cottage by the forest and ran the whole operation—interment, mowing, and maintenance. It was a responsible job, and he was a responsible young man, except for that one night on the bridge that had changed everything.

Now twenty-eight, Charlie had spent his adult years looking after the dead and the living of Waterside. He had sacrificed greatly to keep his word to Sam. He had given up on big dreams of working for the Red Sox front office at Fenway Park or even Major League Baseball on Park Avenue in New York.

Today, like every day, he watched someone weep, and his heart ached. It was always this way. Young, old, healthy, or infirm: They came, they coped, and they moved on.

The woman's knees touched the fresh mound of dirt where he had done his job with the backhoe. Thirty-six inches wide, ninety-six inches long, four feet deep. Eighteen inches of soil on top. All in strict accordance with the laws of the Commonwealth.

The woman tried to stand but wobbled in her heels, then fell back to one knee. This was the moment to offer a hand. Charlie got rid of the Bazooka and moved toward her. He was dressed in the Waterside uniform: a pale blue polo shirt with the cemetery logo, pressed khakis, and work boots.

"Mrs. Phipps?" he said.

She looked up, startled, and seemed to stare right through him.

"It's me," he said.

She shook her head, puzzled.

"It's me, Charlie St. Cloud. Remember? Tenth grade English?"

She wiped her eyes, then nodded. "Of course I remember, but you seem to have forgotten the predicate nominative. The correct syntax is: 'It is I.'"

"I is sorry," Charlie said, his dimple flashing.

Teetering in pointy shoes with a run in her stocking, Ruth Phipps managed a faint smile. Back then she was known as Ruthless Ruth, the terror of Marblehead High, renowned for ruining grade-point averages with her evil pop quizzes and impossible final exams.

"Charlie St. Cloud," she was saying. "Let's see, you got an A on the first test, and then that crash—your brother—"

"That was a long time ago," he said, jamming his hands in his front pockets. "Anyways, I came by to offer my sympathies. And I wanted you to know that you picked one of the most beautiful spots in the cemetery."

She shook her head. "It was just so sudden. So unexpected. I never even had time to say good-bye." Mrs. Phipps wiped the tears from her oval face, and she suddenly seemed human like everyone else. Her arms were as frail as a willow's, her eyes as brown as bark. Death was the great leveler.

"I'm so sorry," Charlie said.

"What's going to happen to me now? What will I do?" Her body was still shaking. "What about my sweet Walter?"

"Trust me," he said. "It's going to be all right. It just takes time. You'll see."

"Are you sure, Charlie?" Her voice was a whisper.

"Not a doubt in my mind."

"You were always such a bright boy. I wondered what happened to you."

"I live over there in that cottage by the forest," he said. "You're welcome anytime."

"That's good to know," she said, pushing a loose strand back in her bun. She straightened her dress and took a few tentative steps on the grass.

"I ought to get going," she said. "Thanks for your help, Charlie."

"My pleasure. That's why I'm here."

Then Mrs. Phipps walked slowly down the hill toward the great iron gates on West Shore Drive.

It was closing time, and Charlie zoomed the utility cart up and down the narrow paths, taking the turns like a grand-prix racer. In his early days on foot, it had taken more than an hour to cover all the acres, looking for mourners lost in thought, picnickers asleep on the lawns, teenagers hiding behind headstones. To speed up this routine over the years, he had modified the little vehicle, secretly adding horsepower and improving the suspension. Now, in the little wagon with WATERSIDE stenciled on both sides, he could secure the grounds in twenty minutes.

He always started at the north end, high on the hill where angels with trumpets alighted on marble, and made his way south across the fields of stone packed in tidy grids. Every pound of granite, every begonia blossom, Charlie thought, was proof of the enduring human need to be remembered. Now he drove along the Vale of Serenity and gazed down at the harbor, where a vintage schooner was sliding into a slip. Then he stopped to greet an elderly gentleman wearing a seersucker suit and wielding a red watering can.

"Evening, Mr. Guidry," Charlie said.

"Well, hello, Charles!" Palmer Guidry said. His hair was wavy and white, and his face was stubbled with an old man's uneven shave. He was one of the so-called cemetery familiars, the regulars who came every day to pull weeds from his wife's grave and wipe dust from her stone. An old cassette recorder playing Brahms was propped against a tree.

"It's closing time," Charlie said. "Can I give you a lift?"

"Why, thank you. So good of you."

Charlie stepped from the cart, shook the old ache out of his knee, and walked toward Mr. Guidry. "Here, let me give you a hand with your things."

It was a conversation repeated almost word for word every evening. Charlie had looked up Mr. Guidry's condition. It was called early-onset Alzheimer's and it afflicted his short-term memory. He couldn't recall yesterday or the day before, but he could still summon images from the distant past. That was why he had no idea he had cleaned his wife Betty's grave the day before, but he could still imagine her in his arms the very first time they danced at the prom. It was why he didn't have a clue that Charlie often picked him up at night but could remember the puzzled look on Betty's face when the stroke rippled through her brain all those years ago.

Mr. Guidry folded his dust rag neatly and tucked it in his

satchel. He switched off the tape player and made one last inspection.

"I love these hollyhocks," he said, running a hand along the crimson bloom of one plant. "You know, they were Betty's favorite."

"I think you told me once," Charlie said, picking up Mr. Guidry's bag and cassette machine.

"Did I ever tell you about the time Betty planted the whole backyard with pink hollyhocks?" he said, tucking the red watering can under his arm and shuffling toward the cart. "They grew seven feet high!"

"I think you mentioned it once."

"Night, Betty," he said, climbing into the front seat. "Sweet dreams, my love. Be back soon."

As they headed down the hill, Mr. Guidry recited the story of the hollyhocks for the thousandth time. Charlie loved the way Mr. Guidry twinkled with each word and how the tears always fell as they passed under the iron gates and made their way onto West Shore.

"Thanks for the story, Mr. Guidry," Charlie said.

"Want to come over for dinner tonight? I'll cook one of Betty's favorites. Finest meat loaf on God's green earth."

"Thanks," Charlie said. "I'd love to, but there's somewhere I have to be."

"Suit yourself," Mr. Guidry said. "You have no idea what you're missing."

He watched Mr. Guidry get into his gold Buick and slowly pull out onto the two-lane road. Then he checked his watch. It was

6:12 P.M. Sundown was exactly thirteen minutes away. The great iron gates creaked as he pushed them shut. It was definitely time to squirt oil in the hinges. Then again, there was something reassuring about the familiar sound.

He turned the big skeleton key in the lock. Waterside was now closed for the night, not to reopen until eight the next morning. He walked back to his cart and sat down in the seat. He looked out across the grounds, where sprinklers were shooting mist into the air.

The serenity around him was palpable. Now he had this paradise to himself; fourteen hours until the world returned. For him, these were the most precious moments. Time for himself. Time to be. Time to think. But most of all, time for his most important activity, hidden deep in the woods.

SEVEN

THE FOREST OF SHADOWS WAS THE LAST UNDEVELOPED
section of Waterside, twenty snarled, tenebrous acres
of oak, hickory, and elm, and very valuable property.
Charlie regularly heard rumors that one developer or
another was panting to snap up the land for condo-
miniums. But this enthusiasm cooled a few months
ago when the real-estate agent died mysteriously and
a prospective buyer collapsed from a brain hemor-
rhage.

Now folks whispered that the woods were
haunted.

Charlie knew better. The forest was the most perfect place in Waterside, and it suited him fine that no
one dared venture into the gloom. On this night, he
steered the cart along the bumpy trail and stopped
next to the blue spruce. A squadron of Canada geese

honked overhead. The light was low, speckling the undergrowth. He checked over his shoulder, a matter of habit. Of course no one was following, but he had to make sure. Absolutely sure.

Then he quickly changed out of his uniform, wadding the pale blue shirt and khakis into a ball and pulling off his boots. He put on an old Celtics sweatshirt, jeans, and running shoes. He reached under his seat, pulled out his baseball glove and ball, and stepped into the woods. No one else would have spotted the slim footpath between the trees. It began on the other side of a rotting log, then widened into a trail that had been tramped down from his walk every night for thirteen years. It followed the line of a little hill to its crest, past a copse of maple trees, then dropped down beside a waterfall and swirling pool.

Charlie, who knew every bump, every vine underfoot, could have run it with his eyes closed. He hurried through the cypress grove that gave way into a clearing. Here was surely the greatest secret of Waterside: a special place he had created with his own hands so many years ago. Back then, he decided to make it the exact replica of the yard at their home on Cloutman's Lane. There was a perfect lawn ninety feet long with a pitcher's mound, rubber, and plate.

He walked to the swings and plunked himself down on one of the wood benches. He kicked his feet up and began to glide. He floated back and forth, and with the breeze beneath him, it felt like flying. Then he leaped from the seat, landed on the ground, and grabbed his mitt. He tossed the ball into the darkening sky. It touched the treetops before dropping back down again. Then he hurled it up once more.

Just as it was about to land in his glove, the wind suddenly gusted and the ball went flying across the field, rolling along the grass, stopping on the edge of the woods. And then a little miracle happened, just as it did every night at sundown.

Sam St. Cloud stepped from the gloom of the forest and picked up the ball. He was unchanged after all these years, still twelve years old with untamed brown curls and a Rawlings baseball mitt under his skinny arm. He wore a Red Sox cap and jersey, baggy shorts, and black high-tops. Oscar sprinted from the undergrowth, tail held high. With soulful eyes and his distinctive yowl, he, too, was the same as before. The dog nipped at Sam's scrawny knees, then yelped at Charlie.

"C'mon, big bro," Sam said with glee, "let's play catch."

A thirty-foot wall of water crashed into the cockpit, knocking Tess from her foot cleats and sweeping her into the lifelines. She gasped for air as the cold ocean wrapped itself around her, sucking her to the brink of oblivion, and then, thank God, her harness and jack line held fast. Moments before, she had zipped into her orange survival suit, essentially a one-person life raft designed for sailing in dangerous weather, enabling her to survive up to a week in the ocean without hypothermia.

Tess coughed up a mouthful of seawater, then pulled herself back to the wheel. *Querencia* was pounding through the howling darkness under bare poles. The main was lashed to the boom, and the decks were cleared.

Giant breaking waves were raging in twenty-second sets, hammering the hull, sending great blasts of spray in the air. Splotches of phosphorus streaked the sky in a stormy fireworks

show. The ocean ahead looked like an endless range of moun-
tains and cliffs rushing toward her at forty miles an hour, and
monstrous peaks collapsed with the force of a landslide.

Tess didn't worry about the blistering wind, the confused sea,
or the salt stinging her eyes. She didn't care about the numbness
in her hands or the pain in her hip from the last fall. She wasn't
alarmed by the radar showing another deep depression building
behind this low. All of her attention—all of her loathing—was focused on one nagging problem: the sloshing seawater in her new
nonslip boots. "Damn," she raged at the ocean. "Five hundred
bucks for this gear, and the damn stuff leaks."

She checked the glowing dials in the binnacle. The anemome-
ter for wind speed showed forty knots, then forty-five. As
Querencia tumbled down the sheer slope of one wave, the
speedometer raced, then climbing the next upsurge, the boat
seemed to stall, threatening to fall backwards into the trough.

Tess braced for the impact of the next breaker. Even as it
slammed the craft, washing her sideways, she held fast to the
wheel. Yes, she hoped, this was definitely good practice for the
Southern Ocean above Antarctica, where she would face blinding
snow squalls and icebergs. That is, if she ever got there. Another
tower of water hit; another blow to her body; but she kept the
boat aimed at the onslaught. It was one of the oldest rules of
foul-weather sailing: Point one small end of the boat into the
waves.

Tess knew there were two good ways to measure nature's
fury. The first was a formula based on the Beaufort Scale, named
after a nineteenth-century British admiral: wind speed plus five,
divided by five. She did the math, and the result was ten. So this

was a Force 10 gale on a scale of 12. All night, the crests had been breaking into spindrift, but now they were toppling, tumbling, and rolling over. That meant only one thing: The storm was gathering strength.

Once before, Tess had made it through a Force 10. It had been on a family outing to the Gulf of Maine, and on that night she had invented her other test of a storm's power. It was less scientific, but just as effective. She called it the Carroll Scale, named after her dad. It involved counting the number of mouthfuls of seawater ingested per wave. Any quantity greater than three meant you were crazy if you didn't seek shelter.

Dangerously close to pitchpoling, *Querencia* was hurtling down the face of a giant wave now at a near-vertical angle. Tess held her breath as she plunged into the trough with the next huge wave rising before her. She heard a loud crack over her head, looked up, and saw that the windex and masthead instruments had blown off. Then the boat broached as the wave smashed the starboard side. She lost control of the wheel, caromed off the cockpit coaming, and skated to the very edge of the boat, now heeling at an extreme angle. Her body was wrapped in the lifelines, and she felt the ocean whooshing inches from her face.

Querencia seemed to be going sideways faster than forwards. The rigging was screaming in the wind. The ocean was almost entirely white. After another mouthful of spray, she knew it was time to go below.

Hand over hand, she climbed uphill to the cockpit. She flipped on the autopilot and adjusted the course to run before the storm. Then she waited for a break in the attacking ocean. She would have only ten seconds to make it inside.

Three... two... one.

She raced forward to the companionway hatch, slid open the cover, and pulled up the washboard. She put both feet on the first ladder step, then fumbled to unhook the tether from the jack line. Her neoprene gloves were thick, her fingers were deadened by the cold, and she couldn't even feel the carabiner. She needed total concentration. The stern began to rise, and there were only seconds before impact.

As a marauding wave overtook the boat, she unfastened the harness and slid inside the cabin, accompanied by a torrent of seawater. With a swift and practiced motion, she jammed the washboard back in its slot and slammed the cover closed.

She waited for a moment in the darkness, listening to the roar outside, the dripping and creaking inside, and the pounding of her heart. *Querencia* was groaning from the relentless attack. She shimmied to port, sat down at the navigation station, and flicked on a light. She unzipped her hood and pulled off her gloves. Her hair was soaked, her face was burning, but there was no point trying to get dry.

She checked the map on her laptop monitor and guesstimated she was a good three hours from landfall in New Hampshire. She reached for the single-sideband radio. It was probably time to give Tink an update. He was at the Marblehead High football game against Beverly, but she would try his cell. She called the marine operator, gave him Tink's number, and waited for the connection. Damn, she would have to admit she had ignored his advice. She had sailed straight into the low. The pressure had dropped so fast her ears had actually popped, and she was stunned to see a reading below 29.4 inches on the barometer. Tink would probably rip her a new one.

Unless she lied.

Tink's voice crackled on the speaker. "How's my girl?" he asked. The roar of the crowd echoed behind him.

The boat lurched violently, but Tess stayed cool. "Everything's great," she said. "Smooth sailing." There was no point telling the truth—it would only make him worry and ruin the game. "Just checking in," she went on, trying to sound unfazed. "Who's winning?"

"The Magicians by one touchdown, and I'm up to hot dog number three." He burped. "How's the weather?"

"Plenty of wind," she said, listening to the hammering waves.

"What about the mainsail?"

"It fits perfectly, with a beautiful flying shape. Tell everyone they did a great job."

"Will do."

"I better run," she said, as the boat pitched forward and plummeted down a steep wave. "I'll call tomorrow."

"Adios, girl. Take care."

Her white lie wouldn't hurt him, she thought. She'd be back in time for supper on Sunday, and he'd never have to know the truth. She shoved the mike back in its cradle, hopped across to the galley, and strapped herself in with the safety belt. She was tired, thirsty, and a bit queasy from the thrashing, but she knew she needed energy. She reached into the icebox and found some fresh lettuce and a bottle of Newman's Own light Italian dressing, but the boat lurched hard, and she decided it was nuts to try cooking. Instead, she pulled a PowerBar from one of the lockers. Her fingers could barely get a grip on the wrapper. She tore it with her teeth and ate it in four bites.

There was nothing to do now but wait. She unhooked herself, made her way forward to the main cabin, and unzipped the top of the survival suit. She climbed into her bunk, cocooned by mesh that held her snugly in place, and began to make a list of all the things she would do when she got back home. Food was uppermost on her list. On the expedition around the world, she would have to subsist on freeze-dried rations and would likely lose the fifteen to twenty pounds that most sailors dropped. During her last week on land, she wanted to splurge. Caramel popcorn and peppermint candy kisses at E. W. Hobbs in Salem Willows. Burgers at Flynnie's on Devereux Beach. Calamari and lobster at the Porthole Pub in Lynn. She grinned at the gluttony. To work off the guilt, she would go on long runs around the lighthouse and take walks with Mom along the Causeway.

And of course, she would visit Dad's grave at Waterside. She had gone there almost every week since he had died two years ago. Sometimes, she stopped by on a morning jog with Bobo. Occasionally, she brought a box lunch from the Driftwood or a cooler of Sam Adams in the late afternoon.

Tess didn't believe in ghosts or spirits. All that psychic stuff on TV was a bunch of hooey for desperate people. It was the feeling of stability that kept her going back, and the serenity. It was a quiet place and beautiful too. Somehow, she felt centered there, and so she went every week to pluck dandelions from the grass or to clip the rosebush that Mom had moved from the backyard.

This time when she got back, she would sit on the bench under the Japanese maple and tell him about her stupid decision to sail right into the storm. She knew wherever he was, he would scold her. Hell, he might yell. But he would never judge her. Despite all her flaws and foolishness, his love had always been unconditional.

Her eyes began to feel heavy, and she was tempted to take a catnap, but suddenly her bunk dropped out from beneath her as the boat plunged into a hole. She floated for a second, then slammed back into the berth. Then *Querencia* broached, lurching violently to one side. Tess was thrown hard against a porthole. She feared the boat had been knocked down flat with its mast in the water, but the weight of the keel rolled the craft back upright. She stepped from the berth and started moving toward the companionway. She needed to see if there was damage to the mast. She zipped up her suit and hood, put the mask in place, and began to climb the steps.

Then the world turned upside down.

EIGHT

IT HAD BEEN THEIR RITUAL FOR THIRTEEN YEARS. AND THEIR secret too. Every evening they came together to play.

Thwack.

Sam caught the ball in his mitt and threw it right back—a two-fingered fastball. It had started long ago on the evening of Sam's funeral after Mom and the other mourners had gone home. As the sun set, Charlie had stayed alone by the grave.

And then, incredibly, impossibly, Sam had appeared from the woods, his body banged up from the crash, still holding his mitt and ball. Oscar was there too.

"What now, big bro?" he had said. "C'mon, let's play catch." The moment had rendered Charlie so distraught—so inconsolable—that doctors gave him powerful drugs to ward off the visions. At first the experts called them dreams, then delusions. The diagnosis: post-traumatic stress disorder. They sent him to a shrink. They gave him Xanax for anxiety, Prozac for depression, and Halcion for sleep. They never believed what he could see.

But see he could, and they were not illusions or hallucinations. He had been dead and was shocked back to life. He had crossed over and come back. He had made a promise to Sam and was given the power to keep it.

A few months later when yet another grown-up refused to believe what he could see, Charlie pretended it was over. He professed the apparitions were gone. So the doctors pronounced him healthy and took him off the medicine. Charlie swore he would never tell another soul about Sam. They'd only call him crazy. They'd never understand. It would be his secret forever. A secret that would govern his days and nights. A secret he would conceal beneath a carefully constructed carapace of charm.

From that day forward, Charlie and Sam played ball each and every evening. Their game at dusk, Charlie believed, was the key to his gift, and he feared that if he missed a single night it would be gone. So he kept careful watch on the angles of the sun. He printed out charts from the Weather Service and tracked the differences between civil, nautical, and astronomical twilight.

As long as they threw the ball every night, he could see Sam, and Sam could see him. Their time together was confined to the Waterside grounds, for Charlie swiftly realized his gift did not extend beyond its walls or gates. So in the mornings, they goofed around on the dock before anyone else was there, and in the evenings, they hung out in the cottage and watched ESPN or James Bond movies. It had worked this way for thirteen years—more than 4,700 nights—and Charlie knew there was no point taking risks.

Over time, he realized his gift had grown, as he began to notice other spirits passing through the cemetery on their way to the next level.

They came in all shapes and for every reason—a crotchety lobsterman who drowned in a squall, a college football linebacker felled by sunstroke, a frazzled hairdresser who slipped on some hair clippings and snapped her neck—but they each shared one telltale trait: they shimmered with an aura of warmth and light. Helping these glowing souls with their transition, he came to think, was his purpose and his punishment.

"So?" Sam said. "How was work today?"

"Pretty good," Charlie said. "Remember Mrs. Phipps? Ruthless Ruth?"

"Yeah, your English teacher?"

"Exactly," Charlie said, floating a knuckleball. "Saw her today."

"Where?"

"Hanging around her grave."

"No way!" Sam said, firing a fastball. *Strike one.* "What happened to her?"

"Heart attack. I think she died while she was getting her teeth cleaned."

"Figures," Sam said. "It was only a matter of time before Dr. Honig killed someone with his stinky breath." His throw sailed high and Charlie leaped to catch it. *Ball one.* For his next pitch, Sam kicked his leg up and zinged a fastball. *Strike two.*

"So how's Mrs. Phipps doing?" he said.

"She's taking it hard. She's flabbergasted by what happened."

"Flabbergast, verb," Sam said, cracking a smile. "Freaking out over how much weight you've gained." Charlie couldn't help laughing. His kid brother was always playing with words.

"So was Mrs. Phipps's makeup all over the place?" Sam asked.

"Yeah."

"Yuck, the new mortician uses too much face junk. He makes everyone look like a clown." Curveball, low and outside. *Ball two*.

"When is Mrs. Phipps crossing over?"

"Not sure. Her husband, Walter, is on the other side. Remember him? The man with no big toe?"

"Oh my God," Sam said. "Yeah, a bluefish bit it off in the bottom of his boat. Remember that stub sticking out of his sandals? It was freaky."

Fastball in the dirt, *ball three*. Full count. Two blue jays shot across the field in little loops. The wind from the ocean rushed up the hill, zigzagged through the tombstones, and swept across the playground.

"C'mon, Sam," Charlie said, smacking his mitt. "It's three and two, a full count. Give me your out pitch."

"Here goes!" He reared up, kicked, and threw a screwball that danced through the air and, in a signature move, actually froze in mid-flight, hovering motionless as if time stopped. Sam snapped his fingers, and the ball blasted off again, making a perfect loop-de-loop before sailing home.

"Steeeeee-rike three," Charlie yelled.

They played ball until it was almost too dark to see, telling each other stories about their day. As a spirit, Sam could have roamed anywhere he wanted, traveling to Alpha Centauri in the Milky Way, shimmering with a rainbow over the Lakes of

Killarney, catching the sun over the Barrier Reef, and riding the moon over Machu Picchu. The possibilities were truly infinite. The known universe with its 40 billion galaxies could have been his playground. And there was heaven waiting for him too.

But Sam had sacrificed all that. He spent his days and nights on Marblehead adventures, sitting behind home plate at Seaside Park for Little League games, sneaking a peek at *Maxim* magazine at Howard's newsstand, and skateboarding down the steepest run on Gingerbread Hill.

"C'mon," Sam said. "Let's go swimming before it's too late. Tag, you're it!"

Then Sam sprinted into the woods with Oscar and Charlie giving chase. Night was almost upon them, the shadows were getting longer, and the forest filled with shouts and yelps. It was the most comforting feeling in the world—the three of them flying through the trees without a care—just as it had been all those years ago on Cloutman's Lane, and just as it would always be.

It happened too fast to brace. Tess suddenly found herself pinned to the ceiling of her boat with bilgewater surging around her head. Radio equipment slammed about, and pots and pans clanked. Chaos resounded inside the cabin. Outside, the ocean and wind roared. Then the lights flickered out.

She heard the sea rushing into the boat, but fear was not foremost in her mind. *Querencia* was built to capsize and right herself. There were pumps onboard to expel the water. In the midst of all the mayhem, she was overwhelmed by something deliciously annoying: the aroma of Newman's Own dressing. The bottle in the galley had obviously shattered, and now the whole cabin smelled like tossed salad.

She huddled on the ceiling, up to her knees and elbows in water, and muttered to the boat, "Please turn back. Come on, come on. Get upright, please?" But nothing happened, so she crawled toward the nav station and found the EPIRB emergency beacon in its bracket. She hated needing help—it was so damn embarrassing—but she pushed down on the yellow power switch, breaking the safety seal, and saw the LED flash. The device was now sending a distress signal via satellite that would ping on every Coast Guard screen in New England. Suddenly she did not feel so alone. But wait, she reminded herself, *Querencia* wasn't sinking, and there was no real need yet for an SOS. Tink and the gang would really bust her chops for crying wolf when she got back to the dock. If the boat started to go down, there would be plenty of time to call the Coast Guard. So Tess flicked the toggle off, and the Mayday light stopped blinking.

A minute went by, then another. The fragrance of Italian dressing was mixing with the sulfuric stench of battery acid leaking from the power units. What was taking the boat so long to roll back over and right herself? The weight of the keel was supposed to pull *Querencia* upright. Her mind jumped to the worstcase scenario. She remembered Tony Bullimore, whose keel was sheared off in sixty-foot seas. He was stranded upside down for five days at the bottom of the world below Australia as his boat slowly sank in freezing waters. "Below forty degrees south, there is no law," he said when he was rescued. "Below fifty degrees south, there is no God."

Tess was not an especially religious woman. She went to the

Old North Church on Sundays largely because it was important to her mother. She was friendly with Reverend Polkinghorne and had built him a sail or two. But she didn't like the conventions of organized faith and she preferred doing it her own way. She considered herself a spiritual person with her own relationship to God.

Now, upside down in the Atlantic, she found herself praying in the darkness. She began by apologizing for her arrogance. She knew she had taken too big a risk. She had been careless, and now she felt ashamed. This wasn't how she wanted it to end, all alone on a weekend sail in a storm that could have been avoided. She prayed to God to be merciful. And then she summoned her father. "Dad, please help me. Tell me what to do." He had always bailed her out of desperate situations. She closed her eyes and promised that if she got back to the harbor she would never do anything so rash again. She would play it safe in the race around the world. She would sail with the rest of the group, even if it meant going slower. She would be a good girl.

Yes, when she got out of this mess, she would go straight to Waterside and take an oath: She would change. Dad had raised her to be bold and to make every moment count, but he would have frowned on her recent recklessness. Flaunting fate was no way to cope with his death.

"Show me the way home," she whispered into the roiling darkness. "Dad, please help me."

NINE

THE DAY WAS GRAY AS GRANITE, AND THE GROUND WAS
soggy from a night of hard rain. The storm had blown
a riot of leaves and branches all over the lawns. Charlie
hid under his yellow hood and looked into the hole
where one of his gravediggers was shoveling. It was
backbreaking work on a normal day, but when the
ground was drenched and the backhoe couldn't maneuver in the muck, it was especially miserable. Now,
compounding the gloom, Elihu Swett, the cemetery
commissioner, had stopped by for a spot inspection.

"The Ferrente funeral party will be here any
minute," Elihu was saying beneath his great umbrella.
He was an elfin man in a tan trench coat, royal-blue
corduroy suit, and rubber galoshes, and his entire
wardrobe appeared to come from the boy's department at Filene's. "How much longer till you're done?"

he asked, taking a sip from a Mountain Dew bottle that seemed half his size.

"Don't worry, we'll be ready," Charlie said, kneeling down and looking into the opening. "How you doing, Joe?"

"Just fine," Joe Carabino said from the bottom of the grave. "But it's Elihu that I'm worried about." He winked.

"What's the matter?" Elihu asked, stepping gingerly toward the hole.

"A lethal dose of caffeine is ten grams," Joe said, leaning on his shovel. "A few more of those Mountain Dews and you'll be pushing up daisies." He paused for dramatic effect. "You feel all right? You seem a little pale." Before Joe could even razz him about his bloodshot eyes, Elihu stuffed the bottle in his coat pocket and took off for his Lincoln Continental. A bona fide hypochondriac, he had been treated by the best doctors in Boston, and every one had urged him to find a new line of work. He refused and insisted on slathering himself with disinfectant and even wearing latex gloves to staff meetings. After all, a good town job was hard to find.

With a swift movement, Joe jumped up from the grave and high-fived Charlie with a muddy hand. "The old lethal-dose-of-caffeine trick," he said. "Poor Elihu, works every time."

Joe was in his early thirties and built like a bull. His blunt face was darkened by the sun, and his thinning hair was teased into a few proud, well-gelled spikes. Male-pattern baldness, he liked to say, was caused by an excess of testosterone, and he had the scientific journals to prove it.

Joe was one of the great rascals of the North Shore. By day, he worked with dirt and the dead. By night, he chased women up and down Cape Ann with a shameless repertoire of strategies and tactics. He had been known to hunt for young widows in the obituaries of the *Marblehead Reporter,* but he wasn't a total rake. He had a code. He steered clear of the bereaved for a minimum of six months—that was the amount of time he heard Oprah say it took to grieve.

Joe's only other great devotion was to his own brand of evangelical atheism. It wasn't enough that he didn't believe in God. He also felt it was his duty to proselytize. That was just fine as long as he kept his missionary work outside the iron gates, but once or twice Charlie caught him grumbling "There is no heaven!" at a graveside service or griping "What a waste!" when a gilded ten-foot cross was brought in by crane to stand atop a mausoleum. Joe the Atheist was duly reprimanded, but it only increased his ardor.

"What's your story tonight?" Joe was asking as they finished dressing the job. "How about coming out with me to happy hour? I'm taking the *Horny Toad* up to Rockport. I know these gals who run a bar there. The things they do, man, you wouldn't believe."

"Give me a hand with the lowering device," Charlie said, walking toward the panel truck on the service road.

"The Dempsey sisters. You ever heard of them?"

"No, never."

"You'd like Nina and Tina. Trust me."

"Let's see how it goes today," Charlie said.

"Yeah, yeah. 'Let's see how it goes.' But when it's quitting time, you'll disappear. Same old story. You know, you should live a little."

Charlie pulled the lowering device from the truck, and the two men carried it across the grass toward the grave. They carefully positioned it over the hole. It was a stainless-steel contraption invented by a mortician named Abraham Frigid, who retired on his royalties to the south of France. In every cemetery around the world, the gizmo was used to lay the dead to rest. With nylon straps and a simple switch, one man could do the work of many and lower a thousand pounds into the earth.

The brilliance of Mr. Frigid's machine was surely in the speed control. Too fast—a quick drop into the ground—and the grieving family would be overcome, the shock too great. Too slow, and the prolonged agony would be insufferable. Thus, Mr. Frigid's eternal contribution: a dignified, emotionally acceptable rate of descent governed by the Galilean principle of inertia and carefully engineered spiral gears, lead weights, and hinges. It was efficient, effective, and relatively painless for all involved.

Charlie heard a horn honk, then saw a procession of cars and one fire engine rolling into the cemetery. He could always tell a lot about a funeral by looking at the vehicles, clothes, casket, and stone. Nice late-model cars, a good coffin, and a big monument meant the deceased had money, but today's burial seemed pretty average. In a few minutes, the vale would be full of mourners. He and Joe had set out one hundred folding chairs and had raised a green tent to cover them. Fortunately, the rain had stopped.

"Work time," Charlie said to Joe. "Let's go."

The funeral director's helmet of black hair was as shiny and sleek as the paint job on her brand-new Cadillac hearse. "How you guys doing?" Myrna Doliber said, slamming the front door shut.

"Better than most," Charlie answered. He had tucked in his shirt and jammed his work gloves in his back pocket. "How 'bout you?"

"Peachy," she said. "Two kids with chicken pox and a third with a busted arm." Myrna's ancestors, the Dolibers, had been the first settlers to arrive on the peninsula back in 1629. Somewhere along the way, they had gotten into the funeral business and ran a monopoly all the way north to Beverly and south to Lynn. On busy days, every Doliber was put to work, even Myrna, who was known as the most superstitious person in Essex County, and who kept a running list of ill omens like a twitch in the left eye or a white moth inside the house.

"Hey, Myrna, I counted thirteen cars in your funeral procession," Joe said with a mischievous grin. "That mean someone's going to die today or something?"

"Knock it off if you want your tip," she said, walking to the tail end of the hearse. She opened the door and stood back. Charlie reached in, released the latch, grabbed a handle of the casket, and rolled it onto the cart.

"Here you go," Myrna said, handing Charlie an envelope. "Don't spend it all in one place." Most funeral directors padded the customer's bill with $100 or more for so-called cemetery gratuities, but then passed only two dollars each to the workers. Myrna was more generous and usually tipped ten dollars.

The two men pushed the coffin across the lawn and stopped beside the grave. Charlie lifted the foot of the box, which was always lighter, and Joe took the heavier head. It was a point of pride: Joe was the strongest worker in Waterside and he liked to show it. They carried the casket and positioned it on the lowering device. Everything was now ready for the funeral.

"Okay," Charlie said. "Break time. I'll catch you later down by the water."

"Ten-four, boss." Joe reached behind his ear for a Camel and strolled down the hill. Charlie walked up the rise and stood under a weeping mulberry for the best view of the proceedings.

Car doors were slamming, and men and women were coming up the hill. Dozens of firefighters in dress uniform stepped from their vehicles. Bagpipes played a wailing song. Charlie watched the tears wash down so many faces. Long ago when he thought he could weep no more over his brother's death, he had investigated the biology of crying. It turned out the muscles above the eyes were responsible, squeezing the lachrymal glands, producing the runoff. Since every adult was made up of about forty-five quarts of water, there was essentially no end to the amount of tears in the world.

He looked over the job one last time. He and Joe had done good work dressing the site, camouflaging the mud pile beneath the carpet of Astroturf and spreading a canopy of roses and carnations around the hole. Now, where was the dead man in the crowd? Often Charlie would see the departed walking the aisles or weaving among the tombstones while the mourners sniffled into their Kleenexes. With their familiar glow, the deceased might sit under a tree or lean against the casket to take notice of who had managed to come for the burial: old girlfriends, office rivals, long-lost cousins. Insincere eulogies could provoke the dead to scoff vociferously and hoot at phony tears. And, more often than not, they would be touched, even surprised, by what their lives had meant to others.

Charlie could always spot the luminous new arrivals. Those who died violently sometimes had scrapes or limped from broken bones. Those who passed away after a long illness were weak and hobbled at first but soon regained their strength and shape. Charlie remembered how banged up Sam had looked after his own funeral, but within days he was back to his old self.

For some, of course, attending their own funeral was too much. At first, they stayed away. Then after a day or two they'd appear at Waterside and make peace with the end. Finally, they'd fade away to heaven, the next level, or wherever they were headed for eternity.

It all depended on how quickly they wanted to let go.

Charlie listened to Father Shattuck begin the ceremony. His few remaining hairs were as white as his collar and had been meticulously spun around his head like a shellacked halo. Only a gravedigger would know the Father's true secret. His dramatic performance was identical every time—all the way to the climactic pauses in Psalm 23 as he walked through the Valley of the Shadow of Death.

I shall fear no evil...

And then, he read from Ecclesiastes. "There is a season for everything," he intoned. "A time for every occupation under heaven. A time for giving birth, a time for dying; a time for planting, a time for uprooting what has been planted; a time for tears, a time for laughter; a time for mourning, a time for dancing; a time for searching, a time for losing; a time for loving, a time for hating..."

And, Charlie thought, a time for new material...

Father Shattuck finished, and Don Woodfin, the chief of the Revere Fire Department, stepped forward. He was a gaunt man with a thick mustache that bridged two hollow cheeks. His dress hat rested on his lanky frame like a cap on a coat rack. "In our 119-year history," he began, "we have suffered six line-of-duty deaths. We gather here today to mark our seventh." He bowed his head. "We thank you, Lord, for the life of a great man. We are grateful for his devotion to a fireman's duty, for his dedication to the preservation of life, and for the way he faced danger."

In the front row, a woman and her baby boy wept. "We ask the comfort of Your blessing upon his family," the chief said. "May they be sustained by good memories, a living hope, the compassion of friends, and the pride of duty well done. And for those who continue to battle the fiery foe, we pray for Your guidance and strength. Keep them safely in Your hands. Amen."

Charlie noticed immediately when a man approached him under the tree. He was wearing a firefighter's dress blues and he seemed lost in thought. There was a faint glow around him that made it clear: He was the dead man, and this was his funeral.

"Can you see me?" the man said after a while.

"Yes," Charlie whispered.

"Are you dead too?"

"No, not yet."

The man scratched his neck. "You look so familiar," he said. His face was grizzled and his voice was as rough as gravel. "Wait," he said, "you're the St. Cloud kid, right? Charlie St. Cloud?" He was pulling off his jacket, rolling up his sleeves, re-

vealing forearms tattooed with images of the Virgin and Child.
"I'm Florio," he said. "Remember me?"

"I'm sorry," Charlie said. "My memory's fuzzy."

Near the grave, the chief was invoking the fireman's prayer.
Florio folded his arms and bowed his head.

> *When I am called to duty, God,*
> *Wherever flames may rage,*
> *Give me strength to save some life*
> *Whatever be its age.*

Then the chief gave his cue, and Charlie stepped forward. He
flipped the jam break on the lowering device. The coffin began its
dignified descent.

Charlie looked at the name carved on the stone.

FLORIO FERRENTE

HUSBAND—FATHER—FIREMAN

1954–2004

And then he realized: Florio was the fireman who'd saved his
life.

The coffin bumped gently to the bottom of the grave. Charlie
pulled the straps and tucked them beneath the Astroturf. Then
he stepped back to the mulberry tree as mourners began to
throw roses onto the casket.

"My God," he said to Florio. "I'm so sorry I didn't recognize you."

"Don't worry," Florio said. "It was a long time ago, and you weren't in very good shape."

"What happened to you? I had no idea—"

"It was an easy two-alarm in a residential unit," he began. "We breached the front door with the battering ram. Rescued a little girl and her mom. Kid was screaming her head off about her cat and dog. So I went back in to get them, and the roof fell in." He gave an uneven smile. "That's it, lights out." He scratched his square chin. "All for a cat and a dog. And you know what? I wouldn't do it any different."

Florio looked across the lawn. "You seen them? A cat and dog? Could've sworn they were here earlier. Running all over the place with a crazy little beagle."

"Wouldn't surprise me," Charlie said. "They may follow you around for a while."

Firemen wiped their eyes with their sleeves. Some crouched in silent prayer. Then the woman came forward, cradling her baby boy.

"My wife, Francesca, and our new son," Florio said. "We tried for years to get pregnant, and it finally happened. God bless them. No better woman on this earth, and Junior is my pride and joy." His voice began to break. "God knows what I'll do without them."

"It's too soon to think about that," Charlie said. "Give it some time."

They watched as his wife and baby left the grave, passed the other mourners, and got into a limousine. Then Charlie began filling the hole, and Florio watched. Shovel after shovel. Dust to dust.

"You know," Florio said after a while, "I've thought about you a lot over the years. I felt so bad I couldn't save your brother. Beat myself up pretty good about that one. I always wondered what happened to you. You married? Any kids? What have you done with your precious life?"

Charlie kept his eyes to the ground. "No wife, no family. I work here and volunteer at the fire station."

"Oh yeah? You a fireman?"

"I got certified as a paramedic. I put in a few nights a month. I'd do more, but I can't go too far from here."

"You know, I was a medic for more than twenty-five years. Seen a lot, but only two or three people ever came back from the dead like you did." He paused. "That was a gift from God, son. God had a reason for saving you. He had a purpose. You ever think about that?"

A long minute passed as Charlie shoved more dirt into the hole. Of course he had thought about that. Every single day of his life, he wondered why he hadn't been taken instead of Sam. What on earth was God's reason? What purpose did He have in mind? Then Florio broke the silence again.

"Don't worry, son," he said. "Sometimes it takes a while to figure things out. But you'll hear the call. You'll know when it's time. And then, you'll be set free."

TEN

THE CORNERS OF HER EYES AND MOUTH WERE FLAKY WITH dried-up salt from the ocean. Tess brushed away the deposits and remembered the last time she had looked like this. No storm had made such markings. Instead, the white residue had been left by the flood of tears after her father's funeral. Back then, her mother had wiped the grains from her face, saying they were a reminder that tears and seawater had mixed together for thousands of years.

Tess also had a whopper of a headache, and her body was black and blue from the battering she had taken. Actually, black and orange would be more accurate, with great blotches of Halloween color everywhere on her arms, hips, and thighs. But the welts and bruises didn't seem to matter just now. What was foremost in her throbbing brain was that she was back on solid ground exactly where she wanted to be: Waterside Cemetery near her father.

She sat in the mottled shade under the maple next to his grave. The lawn was damp, but she didn't mind getting a little wet. She had thrown off her sneakers, rolled up her pants, and was relishing the sensation of just being there in one piece. Her toes wiggled in the grass, and she stretched her legs. She looked down at the granite marker that bore her father's name. She knew she owed her life to him. After that miserable storm, he had guided her home to safe harbor. "You know, I never stopped talking to you out there all night," she said. "You must've heard me."

Of course, she didn't actually believe *he* was right there with her under the tree. That was plain silly, just like the witches in Salem. Dad wasn't lolling around the cemetery, waiting for her to show up. No, he was out there somewhere, a force of energy, or something like that. And if there was a heaven, he was surely sipping beer on some celestial tuna boat, waiting for a strike.

Tess lazed on the lawn, put her hands behind her head, and stared up at the rust-colored leaves. This was the one safe place in the world. The wind was gusting from the north now, and big cauliflower clouds filled the sky, making it one of those rare afternoons in New England, impossibly crisp and fresh, like a Rome apple from Brooksby Farm.

Then an image from last night grabbed hold of her mind: *Querencia* flipping over, the world inverting. "Jesus!" she said out loud, sitting up. She rubbed a bruise on her forearm. She had definitely learned her lesson. Three hours capsized without electricity or radio had scared the hell out of her. Now she had to make good on her promise to her father.

She scooted across the grass and leaned against his stone. It was cool against her sore back and felt good. She turned her head and pressed a cheek against the rock. She ran her fingers along the engraving, where moss was beginning to grow.

GEORGE CARROLL
1941–2002

"I knew you'd come through for me," Tess said with tears welling up. She wiped her eyes and sneezed. She had a simple rule about crying. It went back to childhood. She never let Mom or anyone else see her upset. Weeping was for wimps. But in front of Dad it was different. When she was sad, he never flinched. When she felt weak, he never wavered. In fact, he made her stronger. He had comforted her a zillion times through heartbreak and disappointment. Of course, he didn't always approve of her choices—especially those guys in college who spoke foreign languages and rode motorcycles—but he never judged. He definitely had a temper, especially after a few cocktails, and he wasn't the most introspective or politically enlightened man in the world, but he was the only person who really understood her. No one else came close.

"I promise that I'll change," she said to the stone. "No more crazy stuff on the water. No more daring the Fates. I'll be a good girl." She paused. "I finally scared myself to death."

She rubbed her face, then ran her fingers through her hair. She felt another bump on the back of her head. *Ouch.* It was sensitive to her touch. When did that happen? Must have been when she capsized. The exact details of the night were a blur in her brain, and she still felt rotten from the pummeling waves and noxious fumes of diesel combined with that damn salad dressing. She needed a shower and some sleep. She looked at her hands. Her thumb was banged up, and one nail was broken. An oblong bruise ran the length of her arm. Mom would love that. It was so ladylike.

Tess ran through the list of all the things she needed to do before the starting gun next week. Her first stop on Monday morning would be at Lynn Marine Supply on Front Street. She would give Gus Swanson an earful about that survival gear. Those leaking boots were inexcusable, especially when he charged her full price.

Next, she would have to face Tink in the loft. She dreaded the moment. He would give her the full inquisition, and then they would go stem to stern and tally the damage. Of course, the rigging would need tuning. The storm sail would have to be resewn. The hull might need fresh paint. Her team would have to work overtime to make the repairs in time for the race.

"I know," she said aloud. "It's a waste of hard work and money." That was what really made her feel the worst. Dad had left her a chunk of dough and had urged her to spend it seeing the world. It wasn't much, but he had broken his back saving it, and he wouldn't be happy watching her blow it on repairs. He was an old-fashioned sailor who didn't like expensive fiberglass boats with Kevlar sails. "Sailing," he liked to joke, "is the fine art of getting wet and becoming ill, while going nowhere slowly at great expense." And yet, if the ocean was in your blood—and the two were almost chemically identical, he liked to remind her—you couldn't stop yourself from going to sea no matter how much it cost or how quiet the wind.

She sat silently for a few moments and she could hear his voice. God, how he howled at his own jokes. He would slap his knee, his eyes would squint, and his face and neck would turn red as he unleashed a big laugh. It was only a distant sound in her mind now, gray cells rubbing together, but the memory made everything all right. She waited for more of his laughter—more of that feeling somewhere deep inside. And then suddenly she heard the gunning of an engine and an awful drone. It sounded like a buzz saw. It was coming from just over the hill.

Tess jumped up, her dad's laughter disturbed, and stomped off to see what on earth was causing the ruckus.

What have you done with your precious life? Florio's words had lingered in the air long after he had gone off to the fire station to partake of the wine and cheese reception in his memory. No matter what chores were there to distract Charlie, the question followed. In the Dalrymple family plot, he poured the cement foundation for a new headstone and searched for answers. On the Mount of Memory, he chopped up an oak that had fallen in the storm and he wondered. What had he done with his second chance?

He watched a squadron of geese take flight in a tight V-formation, honking as they cleared the treetops, circling once over the grounds, then winging across the harbor. One thing was for sure: He had spent far too much of his precious life battling those evil creatures. Sure, painters came to Waterside to capture them quaintly on canvas. Old ladies showed up to feed the goslings with bags of crumbs. Little did they know, the gaggle was a public menace. They chomped on grass, devoured flowers, dirtied monuments, and even attacked mourners.

On this fine afternoon, Charlie sat on a bench by the lake with Joe the Atheist, who had invented an ingenious method of scaring off the loathsome birds. It involved deploying an armada of remote-controlled toy motorboats.

"PT-109, ready for attack," Joe said.

Charlie's mind was elsewhere. "You think you'll ever do anything important with your life?" he asked.

"What are you talking about? This is important," Joe said. "We've got a job to do." He looked through a pair of army field glasses and positioned a metal box with a joystick in his lap.

"I'm serious. You think you'll ever amount to anything? You think God has a plan for you?"

"God?" Joe said. "You kidding me? I believe in luck. That's all. You've either got it or you don't. Remember last year? I was one digit away from winning thirty-four mil in the Mass. lottery. You think God had anything to do with that? No way." He shook his head. "Someday, I'll hit it big. Till then, I'm stuck with you." He smiled and leaned forward. "Look! One more squadron of geese at two o'clock by the Isle of Solitude," he said. "Requesting permission to attack."

"Permission granted," Charlie said.

Joe jammed the control stick forward. A gray patrol boat zoomed straight for the birds. The engine blared and a horn hooted. "Two hundred feet and closing," he said, peering through the binoculars. ".08 knots. Target acquired."

As always, the boat worked perfectly. With much panic, the last remaining birds scooted along the water, took flight with a few flaps, and soared over the trees. The little boat banked hard, swooping close to the shore, kicking up a wave of spray. And then Charlie saw a young woman standing on the far side under a willow. She was tall, beautiful, and was waving toward him. She seemed to be shouting, but her words were drowned out by the droning engine. He recognized her from town: It was Tess Carroll, the sail-maker.

"I'll catch you later," he said to Joe, who was focused on maneuvering PT-109 back to its little dock.

"Ten-four," he said.

Charlie jumped in his cart and steered around the lake toward Tess. She was a minor celebrity in town, and truth be told, he had long admired her from afar. They had gone to high school around the same time but she was a couple of years younger. Tess had always been a standout, maybe even a little intimidating, winning races in sail week or campaigning against the local power company's NOx and SOx emissions from its Salem smokestacks. Two years ago, Charlie had buried her father, and she had come just about every week since to pay her respects. She was always alone or with her golden retriever. She never wanted to be disturbed. Joe the Atheist had tried a few times but had gone down in flames, and Charlie knew to stay away.

But there she was now, quite stunning in jeans and a button-down, marching along the path, right toward him, her ponytail sashaying behind. He ran his hands through his hair, wiped his face to make sure there wasn't any lunch still clinging to it, and slowed to a stop. He brushed some crumbs from his chest, tucked in his shirt, stepped out of the cart, and faced her. And as the first words formed on his lips, a pang of self-consciousness punched him deep inside. This uncomfortable, awkward sensation was no stranger: It visited whenever a young woman came to the cemetery, especially one so appealing.

Charlie didn't even have a chance. Before he could say hello, Tess let loose. "God almighty!" she said. "Do you really need to make such a racket? A person comes here for some quiet and what does she get? The invasion of Normandy!"

"Actually, it's our geese-management program," Charlie said, but as the phrase left his lips it sounded funny.

"Geese-management program?" Tess barely contained a guffaw.

"Yes," he said, reflexively, "the Canada geese population—" He stopped mid-sentence. She was staring at him with the most remarkable smile.

"No, go on," she said. "I'm mesmerized. Tell me more about the Canada geese population." She twiddled her ponytail with one hand and tilted her head. That feeling was rising in Charlie— the fizzy mixture of attraction and awkwardness.

"Let me start over. I'm sorry about the noise. We get a little carried away here sometimes." He grinned. "I'm Charlie—"

"St. Cloud," she said. "I remember. Not a Marblehead name, is it?"

"Nope," he said, stunned that she knew him. "It's from Minnesota. Long story."

"Good, I like stories."

"You're Tess Carroll, the one going around the world," he said, a smidge too enthusiastically. He had read about her just the other day in the *Reporter*. A front-page feature had described her solo race, and a color photo had shown her in the cockpit of an Aerodyne 38. "That's some boat you've got," he said. As soon as the phrase left his tongue, he whipped himself for not conjuring something more charming or witty.

"Thanks," she said, pushing a wisp of hair from her eyes. Charlie saw that her thumbnail was black and blue, a hazard of her line of work.

"You sail?" she asked. "Don't think I've seen you on the water."

"Used to. You know, Optimists, 110s. Nothing fancy." Charlie felt that nervous sensation. "Look, I'm sorry we disturbed you. Won't happen again."

"Don't worry about it." She scrunched her face. "I'm just being a pain in the ass today. I've got a killer headache." She rubbed her forehead, and the sun glinted in her eyes.

Charlie lived in a verdant world surrounded by every imaginable shade of green, but for all the moss and bluegrass, he knew this: Her eyes were perfection. Light as lime on the outer edges, rich as emerald toward the center. Transfixed, he found himself saying the opposite of what he intended: "I better go now. Leave you be."

"What's the rush? Another attack on those poor geese?"

Charlie laughed. "Thought you wanted a little quiet, that's all."

"It's better now."

Charlie felt her eyes looking him up and down, and he was

embarrassed about the mud on his boots and the stains on his pants.

"You know," she said, "my dad's buried here. Just on top of that hill." She pointed. "The view's pretty nice up there."

Without another word, she took off, her ponytail bouncing behind her. Charlie wasn't sure whether to follow. Was she inviting him for a look? Or was she finished with the conversation? Every instinct told him to go back to work. He had no business chasing after Tess Carroll. But then he found himself racing up the hill to catch her. When he reached the crest, she had already plopped down on the grass. Her legs were stretched out, and she was looking down toward the harbor where the boats pointed northeast on their moorings. In the distance, a fisherman hauled a lobster pot from the water with a gaff hook.

"Looks like Tim Bird had a good catch today," she said. "His stern sure is riding low."

"Your dad was a lobsterman, wasn't he?" Charlie said.

She looked at him. "Yeah, how'd you know?"

Charlie wasn't sure whether to fess up. He didn't want to seem strange, but he remembered every job he had worked in the cemetery. He recalled every eulogy.

"How'd you know about my dad?" Tess asked again. This time her voice was more insistent.

"I was working the day he was buried."

"Oh." Tess leaned forward and put her face in her hands. She rubbed her forehead and smoothed her hair back. "God, I was in such a fog. Barely remember a thing."

But Charlie recalled the entire funeral and the fact that her dead father hadn't shown up in the cemetery. It wasn't too surprising: Many folks chose to move on immediately to the next level without ever stopping in Waterside.

He studied Tess's face. The memories were coming back now. She was the kind of girl he had dated long ago when everything seemed possible. She was also the kind of woman he never encountered in the graveyard. She had everything going for her—a successful business, a thirty-eight-foot sloop, and those green eyes.

And yet...strangely, she wasn't intimidating at all. She was more lovely, more real than anyone he had known in a long time. That feeling inside was now under control, and he was beginning to feel emboldened. "This may sound weird," he said, "but I loved what you read that day."

"What I read?"

"You know, that poem you recited by the grave."

"You remember?"

"It was e. e. cummings' *dive for dreams*."

"My dad's favorite," she said.

"I went and looked it up afterward." He paused, then recited a few lines:

> *trust your heart*
> *if the seas catch fire*
> *(and live by love*
> *though the stars walk backward)*

"(and live by love," she repeated, "though the stars walk backward)"

"It's great," Charlie said, "but I'm not really sure what that means."

"Me neither."

Her face relaxed, her eyes twinkled, and her lips curled up in a bow. She leaned back and let out a good laugh. It echoed across the grounds, and Charlie was sure it was the best sound he had heard in ages.

Then she rolled over, fixed her eyes on him, and said: "So tell me, Charlie St. Cloud. What's a guy like you doing in a place like this?"

It figured she would spot a cute guy the week before leaving town. That's what had always happened. Her timing was either impeccably off or the guys she liked turned out to be nothing more than deadweight. Tess wanted to live by love, but the stars never walked backward for her, and they most definitely didn't line up for romance. She was unlucky when it came to the heart, always had been, always would be, and that was a big reason she wanted to get away. For her, sailing was a cinch, but relationships were not. Somehow, mastering the wind was always easier than taming unruly men.

And yet, she was lying in the grass and she was kind of— maybe—sort of—liking this guy Charlie. It was strange. She had lived in this town all her life and had never really noticed him until today. Sure, she had seen him around in his blue uniform, but he had always seemed a bit shy, preferring the darkest edges of the local bars and dinner joints. Back at school, everyone had known about the St. Cloud boys. They were the most promising brothers in Essex County until the elder had killed the younger on the General Edwards bridge. It was an accident, a real tragedy, and folks whispered that Charlie had never gotten over it.

But here he was and he seemed perfectly okay. All right, he worked in a cemetery and that was a bit odd, but he was funny, kind, and great looking in that rough way. His arms and shoulders were solid, and he had obviously been working hard that morning. His shirt was damp from labor, his hands were a little muddy, there were flecks of grass in his hair, but damn it if he didn't quote cummings. There was a gentleness to him, a sweetness. And then there was the way he was looking at her.

"Oh, Charlie?" she said. "Quit staring and answer my question."

He blinked. "What question?"

"What're you doing here? Why work in the cemetery?"

"Why not? Beats having an office job. I get to be outdoors all day, plus, I kind of run the place. It's fun being the boss, you know?" He pulled a blade of grass from the lawn, put it between his fingers, cupped his hands, and blew. It made a strange whistle, and suddenly the trees seemed to come alive. This guy was too much. Paul Bunyan in a graveyard. Even the birds sang to him.

She pulled a few blades herself and held them to her face. "Love that smell."

"Me too."

"You'd think they'd bottle it and sell it."

"All you need is some hexanol, methanol, butanone, and—"

"Okay. You talk to the birds. You know the chemicals in grass. Are you for real?"

Charlie laughed. "Of course I am. Real as you are."

Tess studied the dimple on his cheek. The shock of hair flopping down over his eyes. The little slanted scar on his temple. He was real, all right. But then she wondered about him and this netherworld he worked in. "So what about all the dead people?"

"What about them?"

"Isn't it a little creepy, you know, working here every day?"

He laughed. "Not at all. Hospitals and nursing homes deal with death. Funeral homes too. But this is different. This is a park. When folks get here, they're in caskets and urns, and we never even get close to them."

Tess pulled the rubber band from her ponytail. She let her hair fall around her shoulders. Her headache was still there, and she was groggy from the lack of sleep, but she was also feeling more relaxed. She liked the deep timbre of Charlie's voice. She wanted to know more, so she pushed forward. "What about your brother?" she asked.

"My brother? What about him?"

It was almost imperceptible, but she sensed him pulling back.

"He's buried here, isn't he? Is that why you're here?"

Charlie shrugged his shoulders. "It's my job," he said. "Pays the bills and beats selling insurance in an office, know what I mean?" Tess watched his eyes. She knew his answer was just camouflage. This wasn't just any job. He wasn't here to pay the rent.

"Listen," he said. "I've got to get back to work. It's been really nice talking."

"Hey, I'm sorry, that was none of my business. Me and my big mouth."

"Trust me, there's nothing wrong with your mouth," he said. "Maybe we can talk about it another time."

Tess stood and looked up at Charlie. He was more than six feet tall. She wanted to wipe the smudge from his forehead and brush the leaves from his shoulders. But suddenly the intrepid sailor didn't know which way to tack.

"I'd like that," she said. "Another time."

"Hey, good luck with that trip of yours," he said.

"Thanks," she said. "Hope I see you again when I get back."

"Get back?"

"You know, I'm sailing in a few days."

She watched his face closely. His brow furrowed, and then he surprised her.

"Listen, if you don't have plans, how about dinner tonight? I'll throw some fish on the fire."

"You cook too?!"

"Nothing fancy."

Tess couldn't stop the reflex. "Do you always pick up women in the cemetery?"

"Only if they're breathing."

Tess smiled. She liked his guts and she knew exactly what she wanted. "I'd love to," she said.

"Great."

"Can I bring anything?"

"Don't worry, I've got it covered. You drink beer or wine?"

"Take a guess." This was an easy test.

Without hesitating, he said, "Sam Adams all right?"

"Perfect."

"I live over there by the forest," Charlie said, pointing to the thatched-roof cottage with a brick chimney that was nestled against the trees. "I'll meet you at the front gates. Eight o'clock work for you?"

"It's a date."

Tess heard the words—"it's a date"—and couldn't help laughing. Charlie waved, then strolled off toward his cart, leaving her alone on the hill. For months, she had walled herself off from the world with preparations for the race. She had deflected every invitation and dodged every overture. She was the last person in Essex County who was supposed to have a date tonight.

She kneeled down by her father's grave and put one hand on the stone. God, life was strange. Maybe Dad really was looking out for her. He had heard her prayers in the storm. He had guided her home. And maybe he was the reason she found herself saying yes to Charlie St. Cloud's invitation.

"Dad," she whispered into the wind. "Thank you."

ELEVEN

THE SPLASHES OF PURPLE AND PINK PAINTED ACROSS THE sky meant trouble.

For years, Charlie had vigilantly organized his life around the sundown meeting with Sam, and there was no margin for error. He knew that night he had until exactly 6:51 P.M., the precise moment of civil twilight when the center of the sun's disc dropped six degrees below the horizon and the hidden playground was dark. That gave him twenty-one minutes to race around in his old '66 Rambler to pick up swordfish steaks at the Lobster Company in Little Harbor, and then whip over to the other side of town for salad and dessert ingredients at Crosby's.

It was going to be very close.

He thought of Tess standing up there on the hill and couldn't believe his gumption. He had actually asked her to dinner at his place, and her green eyes had lit up when she said yes. Joe the Atheist would be stunned. Had he ever been around a woman like this, so full of spunk and sass? Just talking to her made him feel more alive.

"Relax, you just spent fifteen minutes with her," Charlie told himself. He was a practical man in all matters, including the heart. He had to be. In his life governed by the setting sun, there was no room to get carried away.

Indeed, it had been four years since he had gotten tangled up with anyone. Becca Blint was his last girlfriend. They had met at the Pub at the Landing on beer-tasting night and had fallen for each other over a pint of Angkor Extra Stout from Cambodia. She was a first-grade teacher in Peabody and was funny, flirty, and older. She had definitely taught him a thing or two during their summer together, sprinting through the sprinklers, skinny-dipping in the pond, and snuggling up in the cottage. But when autumn came, Becca wanted to go away on weekends to watch the leaves change or use frequent-flyer miles, jet off to Paris, and visit the Père-Lachaise Cemetery, where Jim Morrison was buried.

Charlie never told her his secret about Sam, and soon his need to be in the graveyard every night at sundown became ridiculous to her. When he had run out of excuses and was exhausted by her nagging, he tried to relax the sunset rule a little, showing up a few minutes late now and then. Nothing terrible happened, so he pushed the limits further. One night, he actually got there after dark, and that's when he realized that Sam was beginning to fade. At first, the change was almost imperceptible, but then it became frighteningly obvious that he was losing his gift. The hard fact was that the more he lived in one world, the less he could see the other.

So he drew the line, retreated to his old ways, and refused to discuss the subject with Becca. When the New Year arrived, she was gone. Charlie found a note pinned to the steering wheel of his cart. *I'm done with this cemetery*, she wrote. *And I'm finished with the living dead. Breaks my heart that I can't be the one to set you free.*

It hurt to see her go, but the choice between Sam and Becca was a no-brainer. He could see no compromise. After that, he protected himself by working even harder and avoiding any real attachments, especially of the female variety.

He kept up the happy-go-lucky appearance and was always first with a joke or quip. But when it came to real entanglements, he had mastered the dodge. Every chance, he sabotaged, and every night, he remembered why. He had robbed Sam of life, so he, Charlie, didn't deserve love or happiness.

The logic was irrefutable.

Now this scary new feeling inside was sounding every alarm. Tess was trouble. If anyone could toss his carefully ordered world upside down, it was she.

He aimed the Rambler into a parking place on Orne Street, glanced at the sky, and checked his watch. Seventeen minutes to go. He got out of the car and saw an energetic woman in a burgundy track suit leading a group of tourists away from Little Harbor, the rocky cove where boat-makers and fishermen had done business for centuries.

Uh-oh. Where to hide?

"Ladies and gentlemen," she bellowed, "please note how our chimneys lean to the east. See? Over there?" She pointed toward a tilting smokestack. "That's because of the sun and the way the mortar dried."

Fraffie Chapman was the town historian and chairwoman of the esteemed Historic District Commission. No citizen could add a cornice or gable or even brick a walk without prior approval of Fraffie's board. Her arched nose was strong, her white hair poofy, and she looked remarkably like one of her direct ancestors: George Washington himself, who had twice visited Marblehead.

"Look at that color," she said rapturously, pointing with her walking stick to the door of an old house. "Gorgeous! Authentic blue. Exactly matches the colonial original!" She took a few more steps. "This way, please. Now, you see those shutters up there! I can't even bear to look." She covered her eyes in mock horror. "They do offend me greatly. Shutters weren't used in the eighteenth century! They came into fashion in the early nineteenth. So, the Historic District Commission is demanding that the owners take down these monstrosities." Charlie laughed to himself. To many townsfolk, the Hysterical Commission was more like it.

"Any questions?!" Fraffie shouted, but the visitors cowered. She turned and stomped toward him. "Marblehead is a clapboard town, not a shingle town," she declared to no one in particular. "We won't let the off islanders turn this into Disneyland. No, we won't!"

Charlie crossed the street to take cover behind a Ford Explorer. Maybe he could avoid her. But then he heard her piercing voice: "I see you, St. Cloud! You can't hide from me!"

She frowned, cocked her head, and marched over to him. "You better cut those bushes on West Shore. I'm serious this time. Get them in shape or face my wrath!"

Charlie preferred letting the boxwood and yew in front of the cemetery grow wild. They made the entrance feel more natural. But he didn't have time to argue. He could tell from the low light reflecting on the water that the sun had already dipped below the tree line.

"Those bushes aren't historical," Fraffie intoned. "They're a blight. I'm giving you one more chance. Remove them or we'll go to war."

Charlie imagined her shooting him with her very own musket or slashing him with a cutlass. Then he mustered his most polite tone. "I'll see what I can do; now, excuse me please. I'm in a hurry."

Fraffie turned back to her group and pointed her cane toward the waterfront. "That's Gerry Island out in the harbor. Elbridge Gerry was our most famous native son. He was Vice President of the United States in 1813, and we named a school, a street, and a veteran fireman's association after him. . . ."

Off Fraffie went, declaiming about pitched roofs and paired chimneys. Charlie rushed down the street and opened the door to the Lobster Company, with its sign in the window: UN-ATTENDED CHILDREN WILL BE SOLD AS SLAVES. He stepped inside and was accosted by the musty smell of brine and fish. Big tanks filled with lobsters gurgled in the middle of the room. The concrete floor was wet from water splashing over the edges. As a boy, he had loved pushing his face up against the moist glass and watching the crustaceans do battle.

At the register, a pale man in pinstripes was collecting his purchase. Pete Kiley had played second base on the high-school team and was now an associate in a fancy Boston law firm. He and Charlie had turned more double plays than any infield in Marblehead history. Now Pete and his family lived out on the Neck in an expensive home and took vacations in France and Italy.

"Hey," Pete said, turning around. "I'll be damned. If it isn't number twenty-four...shortstop...Charlie St.—"

His routine was always the same no matter where they ran into each other, and Charlie knew it was intended to cut through the awkwardness. Pete had done something with his life, and Charlie hadn't. But the truth was that Pete's attempt to recall their glory days only made things feel worse.

"Sorry I can't stay and chat," Pete said, twirling his BMW keys, "but the wife is waiting for me in the car." He punched Charlie in the shoulder. "Give me a ring one of these days, and we'll have you over for dinner. It's been too long."

"You bet," Charlie said, watching him go. Of course, he would never make the call.

"That kid's making too much money," an old voice said behind the counter. "Just shows you, taxes should be higher on the rich." Bowdy Cartwright had owned the Lobster Company forever. He was a jowly fellow with at least three chins who had amused generations of kids with his uncanny imitation of a puffer fish. "What are you looking for today?" he asked. "We've got good haddock for chowder and clams for steamers with drawn broth—"

"I'll take two swordfish steaks, half a pound each."

"You got it. Just off the boat from the Grand Banks."

A young woman stepped out from one of the back rooms of the store. Margie Cartwright flipped her long blond hair to one side and flashed a red lipsticky smile. She went straight to the cash register, leaned over, and thrust her cheek toward him.

"Come on, Charlie. Give one up for your old gal."

Way back before he ruined everything, Margie was his sweetheart. She was a year older. He was a sophomore, she was a junior, and they had met one freezing Thanksgiving at the big game against Swampscott. She was a cheerleader who insisted on wearing a little skirt and sweater whatever the weather. After all, she said, girls with pompoms had no business in parkas and long pants. Their romance was innocent enough, with nights spent immersed in conversation over chicken parm at the House of Pizza. Then came the accident, and Charlie retreated. All the cheerleading in the world would not lift his spirits. Margie tried her hardest to bring him back, but he pushed her away.

Charlie leaned forward and kissed her.

"Thatta boy," she said, batting long eyelashes. Charlie smelled her Chloe perfume. In many ways, Margie hadn't let go of her glory years. Her long blond hair was unchanged, and she wore a tight pink sweater, short black skirt, and high boots. Up and down the coast, the fishermen knew her name and outfits, her only form of protest against spending her life in the family's fish shack.

"So? Whatcha cooking tonight?" she asked.

"Oh, nothing much."

"Here ya go," Bowdy said, handing Charlie a paper bag. "That's two swordfish steaks, Margie. A little more than a pound."

"Two steaks? Oh really!" Margie said, arching a well-plucked eyebrow. "Fish for two?"

"Nah..."

"C'mon, Charlie! Who is she? Maybe I can put in a good word for you."

Charlie threw a $20 bill on the register. "Sorry, Margie. I gotta run. Ring me up, please."

"You're no fun anymore. What's the big secret? You know I'm going to find out anyway! Might as well tell me."

Charlie thought for a moment. She was right. Her far-flung network of spies would report back within days. What was the harm in telling? She knew the skinny on every person in town. In fact, maybe she could help.

He checked his watch—eleven minutes to go—and decided to skip Crosby's for salad and dessert. If he improvised at home and whipped up something from scratch, he still had a few minutes to get some valuable intelligence. So he leaned forward conspiratorially, and said, "Swear you won't tell?"

"Cross my Catholic heart."

"All right," he said, lowering his voice. "What do you know about Tess Carroll?"

TWELVE

Tess leaned forward and peered into her grandmother's soft green eyes. The old woman was sitting
in a brown recliner near a window in the Devereux
House nursing home. Tess had walked over on her
way home from the cemetery and had immediately
noticed that the smell of medicine and disinfectant
was stronger than ever in the long green hallway leading to Room 216.

"Nana, it's me," Tess said. "You won't believe it. I
think I just met a great guy!"

Her grandmother blinked and stared straight
ahead at the TV. *Walker, Texas Ranger* was on, and she
made a habit of watching every day. Her wrinkled
hand fumbled for an orange-juice carton with a straw.
She lifted it up, and took a sip without saying a word.

Tess was Theresa Francis Carroll's namesake and she had always been able to count on her grandmother's care and wisdom when she was bounced by some of life's unavoidable speed bumps. In fact, she had come to Nana for consolation after Scotty McLaughlin had dumped her at the Corinthian Club on New Year's Eve in 2000. A romantic at heart, Nana never had an easy life. At nineteen, she married a dashing lobsterman from the rival town of Nahant and was already pregnant when he vanished in a nor'easter. "No one could compare," she told Tess and so despite a long line of suitors, she never remarried. Her life story, repeated dozens of times, always made Tess cry. "Wait for your true love," Nana admonished. "Never settle."

From her grandmother, Tess had learned what it meant to be a survivor. To support her infant son, Nana had gone to work in the shoe factories in Lynn. Her whole life had been a struggle and, at eighty-six, the fight was still in her after an eleven-year battle with lung cancer. Twice before, doctors had taken extraordinary measures to bring her back from death's door, and each time there was a little less of her left. Now the small sign next to her bed said simply: DNR—DO NOT RESUSCITATE.

And yet, in Tess's mind, Nana was still indomitable. She was a diehard Democrat who kept a crumpled, yellowing *Boston Globe* picture of the three young Kennedy brothers on her mantel. She loved to gossip about the men in town, and she insisted—outrageously—on smoking Marlboro Reds even after her health had given way.

Some days, she recognized Tess. Most days, she mistook her for her older sister who had passed away the day George Bush defeated Michael Dukakis by 325 electoral votes. On occasion, it seemed as if she didn't even see Tess at all. She just gazed into space with those soft eyes. Her one stab at dignity was her insistence on being dressed every day in a colorful hat and cheerful jewelry from the dime store.

Now she sat frozen in her recliner, humming and staring out the window.

"What are you searching for out there?" Tess asked. The view from Devereux House looked out on an asphalt parking lot, where Tess saw a bird on a fence.

"Are you looking at that sparrow? Is that what you see?"

Nana smiled, closed her eyes for a moment, then opened them again.

"So what have you been up to?" Tess asked. "Is Mr. Purdy still chasing you around the rec room? You told me he's a real pervert." Again, silence.

So this is what it came down to. A long life, and now this? Years alone in a fog. Tess swore she wouldn't allow herself to end up this way. She would go out in a blaze of glory. She never wanted to fade away. That was the worst thing that could happen.

"Listen, Nana, I came to say good-bye," Tess said. "Remember? I'm going on a big sail all the way around the world." She paused and looked at her grandmother's beaded necklace. "I'll bring back jewels from the Orient. How's that sound?"

Nana's lips curled up. There was a little twinkle in her eye. Tess wondered what she was thinking. Could she even hear any of this?

"You know I'm here, don't you?" Tess said. "You know I'm right next to you."

The room was silent. Nana's mouth pursed, her wrinkles radiated, and then she finally spoke in a firm voice: "Of course I do."

It was the first time in months she had acknowledged her presence. Tess was speechless.

"You all right, honey?" Nana said.

Tess couldn't find words.

Nana's eyes focused and she said, "It's okay, dear. Everything's going to be all right, and I'll see you very soon."

Then Nana's lids closed, and her head began to tilt. Soon she was snoring softly. Tess got up and kissed her grandmother's powdery cheek.

"Love you," she said. "See you soon."

THIRTEEN

CHARLIE LET GO OF THE ROPE AND FLEW THROUGH THE
air. He tucked into the cannonball position, held his
breath, and splashed into the cool water. With a few
good kicks, he swam to the mossy bottom, grabbed
hold of the big boulder to keep himself down, and listened to the sound of crackling air bubbles and his
pounding heart.

He had made it to the forest before sundown with
only seconds to spare, but now for the first time, he
faced unfamiliar feelings about being there. Conflict-
ing ideas were washing around in his brain: He imagined borrowing Joe's boat and whisking Tess away on
a sunset cruise around the harbor, uncorking a good
bottle of wine, then motoring over to Manchester for
dinner.

But that wasn't an option. He had a promise to

keep and a ritual to perform. First, he and Sam played catch in the clearing, then they jumped into the little pond he had dug with his own hands all those years ago. Charlie had copied every detail from the swimming hole on Cat Island. The dimensions were exactly the same; the braided rope was nearly identical; and the big knot at the end was triple-tied. Those days at YMCA summer camp had been the happiest ever, crammed with afternoons racing Widgeons and Ospreys, and evenings diving from the old rope.

When his lungs began to burn, he let go of the boulder and pushed off the bottom. He broke the surface with a great splash, and when the ripples settled, he heard Sam's voice on the bank: "One minute and twenty-two seconds! Charlie St. Cloud shatters the Waterside record!" His brother was sitting shirtless on a log with Oscar, who was busy scratching himself. There were fleas in the afterlife too.

It was just past sundown in the Forest of Shadows, and soft streams of violet light filtered through the trees. Charlie climbed out of the pond and wrapped a towel around his shoulders. His dripping cutoffs were loose on his narrow waist and hung low on his hips. The shorts touched his knees, where scars from the accident crisscrossed in fading stripes. He swept his hands over his chest and stomach, skimming off extra water, and shook out his hair, spraying Oscar.

"You see Tiny Tim down there?" Sam asked.

"Nope," Charlie said. "No sign of him." Tiny Tim was the turtle who lived in the pond. Thirteen years ago, the boys had plucked him from the little tank near the cash register at Animal Krackers in Gloucester. When Charlie had moved to Waterside,

Tiny had come along too. With plenty of food and his own pond, he had grown into a giant.

Sam scratched his head. "You think he met a hot reptile babe and took off?"

"Doubt it."

"Wouldn't blame him, would you?" Sam said. "Pretty small pond for a guy his size."

Charlie glanced at his watch. Tess would arrive at the great iron gates in sixty minutes. He knew he had to get back to the cottage, hide all the piles of newspapers, throw the dishes in the washer, and get the coals fired up.

"Time for one more dive," Charlie said. "Go for it, little man."

With a gangly arm, Sam reached for the rope. He wore jean cutoffs, too, just like his older brother, and was so skinny he seemed to be all knobs and joints—elbows, knees, shoulders, ankles. "Give me a push."

Charlie obliged, and Sam swung low across the water, then arced upward. At the perfect moment, he let go. Like a leaf on the wind, he soared up and up, defying gravity. Then he tucked into a front somersault with a 540-degree spin, an extreme maneuver he had seen on ESPN's Summer X Games.

Sploosh.

He disappeared underwater for the longest time, and when he finally surfaced, he had a big smile. "Tiny says 'hi!' He's cool. He's not going anywhere." Sam climbed out of the pond and grabbed his towel. "You want to try a misty flip?" he asked.

"No way. Too hard."

"Chicken."

"Chicken? You've got a few advantages in the flying department."

"Don't be a wimp," Sam said. "It's easy. I'll show you how. It won't kill you."

"Nah," Charlie said. "I'm done." He pulled a Salem State Vikings sweatshirt over his head.

"What's up with you tonight?" Sam said. "We barely even threw the ball around, and now you're splitting?"

"Nothing's up."

"Yeah, right. You're acting all freaky."

"No, I'm not."

"Are too."

"Enough, Sam."

Charlie slipped on a running shoe and tied the laces. He hated being impatient with his brother, but he was tired of the same old routine.

Sam's eyes widened. "Wait a minute! It's a girl, right? You met someone. You've got a date tonight!"

"What are you talking about?"

"Liar!" Sam said. His brown eyes were full of glee. "Tell the truth. Resistance is futile. What's her name?!"

Charlie pulled on the other shoe and tried an evasive tactic. "I've got a new nomination for the all-time greatest Red Sox team," he began. "Luis Tiant belongs on our list with Boggs, Yastrzemski, Garciaparra, Young..."

"Nice try," Sam interrupted. "You think I'm falling for that?" He grinned triumphantly. "Spill already! What's her name?!"

"Give me a break," Charlie said.

But like any twelve-year-old who could be a brat if he chose to, Sam would not stop. "You must really like her if you're trying to hide her," he said.

In that moment, Charlie made a quick calculation. He knew how these conversations had always gone. Above all, he figured he would get home faster if he just surrendered to the cross-examination.

"Her name is Tess," he said finally.

"Tess who?"

"Tess Carroll."

"What else?"

"She's a sail-maker. Her dad died a couple of years ago from a heart attack."

Sam was sitting right beside him on the log. He stared at his brother, and asked, "Does she like the Sox?"

"Don't know yet."

"So what's the matter? What are you so afraid of?"

"Not afraid of anything." Another lie. Of course, he was petrified.

Sam smiled and put on his T-shirt. "I can do recon, if you want. See if she has a boyfriend."

"Margie Cartwright says she's single."

"So how can I help?"

"Stay out of it." Charlie's tone was firm.

"C'mon, can't I have any fun? You know, like go through her underwear."

"No, Sam. No panty raids." He checked his watch. "Whoa, it's late. I better get going." He stood up from the log. "Remember," he said, "no monkey business. Stay away from Tess and keep clear of the cottage tonight."

"Relax, you're too uptight," Sam said, reaching for the rope and stepping onto the knot. "I promise I won't stink up the place."

"But flatulence is one of your specialties."

"Flatulence, noun," Sam said with a grin. "The ambulance that scoops you up when you're squashed by a steamroller." He let out a great laugh. "Give me a push, big bro."

Once more, Charlie obliged, and Sam swung out over the pond. He glided back and forth a few times, picking up speed, and then, at the perfect moment, he let go. "See you later."

Charlie blinked, Sam vanished, and all that was left in the Forest of Shadows was the fading light and the whoosh of the wind.

FOURTEEN

Tink had already plowed through a pint of Ben & Jerry's Chubby Hubby and was halfway through a triple-decker baloney, Swiss, and slaw sandwich. A giant bottle of Diet Dr Pepper, his only nod to weight-watching, sat with the remains of his trencherman's snack on the bench in Crocker Park. Tess's dog, Bobo, lazed in the grass nearby, chomping through a bag of sourdough pretzels.

He had come to hang out here on the bluff above the harbor as day turned to night. An hour earlier, he had swung by Lookout Court to check on Tess's place while she was away and to make sure everything was all right. So he had let himself in the front door that was always unlocked and had seen the usual mayhem of her whirlwind. Running shoes caked with mud strewn in the living room, a jogging bra hanging from the kitchen doorknob, dishes and pans piled in the sink clamoring for cleaning, and Bobo whimpering to go outside.

So as he often did, he took the golden retriever to the park. That was the extent of his romantic life these days. High school ball games with the guys. Movies at the Liberty Tree Mall in Danvers. Long nights on the stool at Maddie's. And, always, good old Bobo.

Now Saturday night was already upon him, and once more he had nothing much to do. Some weekends, he managed to score a meal off Tess by dropping by and pleading hunger. If she was home, she always took him in and they wound up cooking together, renting a Steve McQueen movie, and lazing on her shaggy sofa. Sure, she managed to burn everything she ever touched in the kitchen, but he didn't mind. He just liked being near her.

On one hand, Tess was like his kid sister. She was the type of girl who needed a big brother to keep her on the straight and narrow. She was smarter than everyone else and as strong a sailor as anyone he had ever met. But she also needed an anchor after her dad had died, and he was trying his hardest to fill that job.

To be totally honest, since the moment they had met at the Topsfield Fair, he'd wrestled with a wicked crush on her. At the time, he was a small-time celebrity, doing the weather on TV, and had volunteered to sit in the dunking booth to raise money for the Jimmy Fund. A stunning woman with long dark hair had fired three footballs at the target. Each spiral found its mark, plunging him into the murky tank. When he dried off, he was determined to meet the girl with the killer arm.

That was four years ago, before he was run off the air for his wiseacre remarks about Skeletor the Anchorwoman. Tess had written the station on his behalf; they had become fast friends; and he had gone to work for her in the sail loft. Every minute of every day, he tried to conceal his ardor, all the while hoping she would fall for him. He had even tried dropping some pounds to make her take notice, giving up his beloved Chubby Hubby. In the end, though, it wasn't his potbelly that was getting in the way. When it came to men, she was a mystery. There was no holding on to her. She was a free spirit, and he lived uncomfortably with his longing.

Bobo was eyeing his triple-decker now, and Tink pulled out a slice of baloney and tossed it to him. "So what's the girl up to?" he asked. "She got a hot date tonight?" The dog woofed. "Figures."

Tink hated that this would be his life for so many months while Tess was sailing around the world. He got up from the bench, wiped the mustard from his beard, and tucked in his flannel shirt.

"Time to go, boy," he said, snapping the leash on Bobo. He tossed the trash in the can, and they lumbered down Darling Street. Ahead, he saw the steady stream of Saturday night traffic on Washington. He trudged up the hill toward Abbot Hall, cut into the square, and saw a pretty woman in front of a pale blue saltbox.

La-Dee-Da Channing was sitting on her stoop, filing her nails, lost in *InStyle* magazine. A fancy green scarf was tied around her head, and she was wearing Jackie O shades even at dusk. La was an aspiring actress who didn't let her administrative post in the harbormaster's office keep her from dressing for Tinseltown.

"Evening," he said.

La didn't even look up. "Brad and Jennifer practice Bikram yoga together," she said.

"Huh?"

"Brad Pitt and Jennifer Aniston. All the stars do yoga in a heated room."

"Whatever happened to jogging?"

La looked up and focused on his belly. "You tell me."

"Ouch," he said, patting his prodigious tummy.

"You look great tonight," she said. "You even took a bath."

"Thanks," Tink said, feeling his chest puff out. "Everybody washes on Saturday."

"Not you," she laughed. "Bobo!" She leaned forward toward the retriever. "Here, boy."

Tink shrank, watching her rub the dog's ears. "You going to Maddie's later?" he asked.

"You buying?"

"Anything for you, La."

"Awww, what a sweetheart." She lowered her glasses, and her brown eyes gave him a long look. Just when all seemed lost for the night, Tink felt a glimmer of hope. "See you at Maddie's," he said, tugging on Bobo's leash. "Maybe afterward we can try some of that yogurt stuff."

"Yoga, you goof!"

"I'll be Bob and you can be Jennifer."

"Brad," she laughed. "Better watch out or you might get hurt."

"No chance. You have no idea what this hunk of burning love can do," he said. "Just wait, it'll blow your mind."

FIFTEEN

TESS WAS FEELING STUFFED AND EVEN A LITTLE TIPSY, BUT she agreed to another Sam Adams. Her appetite was back, and the brew had numbed her killer headache. She still had those sea legs from the storm, but Charlie had pulled out all the stops for dinner, and she was enjoying every moment. His grilled swordfish with tomato and capers had been sublime, and the salad of beets and oranges was heavenly. She definitely had no room left for dessert. But she would find a way.

They were seated at a little round table on the edge of his living room. The lights were low, a log crackled in the fireplace, and two candles framed his face. He was telling her a story about his surname, which came from St. Cloud, Minnesota, the Mississippi River town where his mother was born and from which she escaped as soon as she could. The original St. Cloud, he explained, was a sixth-century French prince who renounced the world to serve God after his brothers were murdered by an evil uncle. Tess watched his mouth move and listened to his beautiful, deep voice. Then, seamlessly, he was delving into something called nephology, the scientific study of clouds, based on the Greek *nephos*. There were nine types, he said, each defined by appearance and altitude. He was full of strange and wonderful facts, and his mind worked fast, making the most unusual leaps. She sipped on her beer, stared into his eyes, listened some more, and felt her edges begin to soften.

She always hated guys who fussed over her with fancy dates to Boston including five-star restaurants and valet parking. They ordered vintage wine, waxed on about white truffles, and blabbed endlessly about themselves with the preposterous hope of luring her into bed. They were predictable, insincere, and boring.

Charlie was different. He was like some rare and exotic animal—a gentler, more sophisticated breed than the critters she had grown up around. There was also something effortless about the evening. For starters, there wasn't a cookbook in sight. He did it all himself—sautéing, flambéing, and all those other unfathomable activities in the kitchen that she had no idea about. But what struck her the most wasn't what Charlie had to say about cirrostratus clouds. It was how he listened. He seemed to absorb every single word that came from her, and tonight, feeling as comfortable as she did, there were many of them.

"I really love the name of your boat," he was saying. "*Querencia*, right?"

"Yes," she said. "You speak Spanish?"

"No, but I read a book about bullfighting once. Isn't that the spot in the ring where the bull feels protected and secure?"

"Exactly," she said. "Sometimes it's a place in the sun. Other times it's in the shade. It's where the bull goes between charges. It's like an invisible fortress, the only safe place."

"Just like your boat."

"Yeah, and just like Marblehead."

Soon, Tess found herself wanting Charlie to know everything about her. She wanted him to know how she had broken her arm riding a bike on the Causeway when she was eleven. She wanted him to know how Willy Grace, her first boyfriend, had tricked her into a camp-out on Brown's Island when he had a lot more than stargazing on his mind. She wanted him to know how she had always slow-danced to the fast part of "Stairway to Heaven." And she wanted him to know more about her dad, who for some reason tonight felt closer than ever.

Yes, Tess felt a rare connection to Charlie, and it was at once exciting and frightening. With every passing moment, she knew that she was losing a little bit of control and that wasn't good. Everything about him was like a gentle undertow pulling her deeper and deeper. But she was leaving in less than a week, and no good-looking, great-cooking, careful-listening guy was going to sink her.

"Want dessert?" he said all of a sudden.

"Do I look like a girl who ever says no to dessert?"

"Coming right up," he said, gathering the dishes.

"Better be good." She sat back in her chair and admired the way he walked into the kitchen. He was wearing 501 jeans, and

she could just make out the impressive cuts of his deltoids and tri-
ceps under his sweater. "You sure I can't help with anything? I feel
like a lump just sitting here."

"Make yourself useful and change the CD."

"Any requests?"

"Nope, it's a test."

Tess looked around for the stereo. The room was wonderfully
dark and warm. Rough-hewn beams ran the length of the ceiling.
Antique maps and framed black-and-white photographs punctu-
ated the walls. Piles of books were everywhere—crammed into
shelves, stacked on the floor, or heaped atop rugged old furniture
made of wood and leather. The place felt like a secret hideaway,
so safe and cozy that you'd never want to leave.

On a stand in the corner, the stereo was playing the blues,
something vaguely familiar on the guitar, maybe Muddy Waters,
but that seemed too predictable for him. She was sure he had
picked something special and different for the evening, even if she
wasn't sophisticated enough to recognize it.

Looking over his stacks of CDs, she felt a twinge of pressure.
What if he didn't like what she chose? She thumbed through a
few, all the latest stuff: Cornershop, Wilco, the Magnetic Fields.
She saw the Jayhawks and slipped *Hollywood Town Hall* into the
machine. The Minnesota band felt just right: not too predictable
or noisy, with a few jangly ballads.

"Not bad. You can stay," Charlie said, emerging from the
kitchen with a chocolate cake and candle.

"Wow! What's the occasion?" she said.

"Your birthday."

"But it's not till February."

"September, February, whatever. I thought we should celebrate early because you're going to be away." He held the cake forward so she could blow out the candle.

In that moment, Tess almost melted, but something inside told her to be on guard. She carefully took his measure. He was standing there all tall and handsome, with the candle flickering in his eyes. His dimple danced on one cheek, and the cake itself seemed miniature in his large hands.

"Go on," he said, "what're you waiting for? Make a wish!"

Was he pulling her leg? No one on planet Earth was that sweet. She took a breath, wished for him to be as perfect as he seemed, and was about to puff out the candle when he busted up laughing. "You totally fell for it, didn't you?" he said.

Tess couldn't help giggling too. "Yes, I did," she said. She poked one finger into the icing. "Tell the truth. Why the cake?"

"It's the anniversary of Ted Williams hitting .406."

"You're kidding."

"Nope," Charlie said, setting down the cake. "This week in 1941, Teddy Ballgame played a doubleheader and went six for eight. The guy was only twenty-three years old."

"Oh no," she said. "A Red Sox fan."

"You?"

"Hate baseball. It's so boring, I call it standball. You know, they just stand around for nine innings. Football is more my speed, and the Patriots are my guys."

"Really?" he said, a bit incredulous. "I didn't figure you going for guys with no necks."

"Oh yeah, big time, and the hairier the better."

With that, Tess suddenly felt relieved. The bubble had burst.

They didn't agree on everything, and that brought a curious comfort. He wasn't perfect after all. Football vs. baseball. Sure, it was trivial, but that was beside the point. Then she realized she was actually keeping score. Normally she didn't really notice what guys thought about things. But here she was regretting that she hadn't followed the Sox box scores since Dad had died.

He handed her a piece of cake, and she took a bite. She closed her eyes and said nothing.

"It's okay, right?" Charlie said. "I ran out of time and threw it together."

"It's edible," she said, rolling the chocolate over her tongue. She was working it—and Charlie—which she enjoyed. Finally, she smiled. "Actually, it's wonderful. Like everything tonight." She stopped, studied her Sam Adams and realized it had to be the beer talking now.

"You like to cook?" Charlie asked.

"No, I like to eat," she said, slowly savoring another bite. "I make a mean Jell-O and I'm huge with the mac and cheese, but other than that, I'm pretty useless." A third bite. "The worst part of solo sailing is the food. Miserable freeze-dried rations." A fourth bite.

"Slow down," he said. "I only made one cake."

She grinned. Why did dessert even taste different tonight? Maybe it was Charlie, a guy who even made food better.

"So where'd you learn to cook?" she said. "Your mom?" The question had a little edge: If he was a mama's boy, it might take some more luster off him.

"Yup, my mom," he said, without hesitation. "I called her in Oregon to get some ideas for tonight. Know what? She was appalled that I wasn't taking you out to dinner on our first date. She warned me it was a big mistake and said I'd give you food poisoning." He winked. "Thank God, I don't always listen."

"Not so fast. I think my stomach feels upset."

"I hear booze kills the bugs. How about another beer?"

"You trying to get me drunk?"

"Definitely," he said, disappearing again into the kitchen.

"Well, I can outdrink you and outeat you. Bring it on," she said. He had passed yet another test. He wasn't embarrassed to be close to his mother, but it also sounded like there was a healthy distance between them, and that must have been hard to figure out after the accident.

"So what's your mom doing in Oregon?"

"She moved out there right after the accident," Charlie called back. "She didn't want any reminders. She's got a new life now. She's married with stepkids."

"You mean she just left you here?"

"No, I refused to go. So I lived with the Ingalls family till I graduated. Since then, I've been on my own."

Tess got up from the table, walked over to a darkened corner of the room with maps on the wall, and switched on a lamp. The charts were tacked up with pins, and they showed the roads and waters of the Eastern seaboard. Tess noticed strange concentric circles drawn neatly on each of them. The rings spread out from Marblehead and reached all the way to New York and Canada. Next to the maps, there were tables listing the exact times of the sunrise and sunset for every day of the month.

"What are these about?" she asked when Charlie returned.

She put a finger on one of the loops. "I know it's got something to do with distance, but I can't figure it out."

"It's just a project of mine," he said, delivering a beer and going to the other side of the room. "Now, tell me more about this trip of yours."

"What about it?"

"For starters, your route?"

"Okay, I start in Boston Harbor on Friday, then head south to the Caribbean, and eventually go through the Panama Canal."

"Show me." He was standing in front of a big antique map that was framed behind glass. Tess walked toward him. She was feeling warm, so she pulled the button-down up over her head and threw it on the couch. She was wearing a white tank top underneath, and she could tell his eyes were following her hands as she fixed the bra strap that was poking out. Then she took a few more steps and stopped next to him.

"You're limping," he said. It was a cute attempt to cover for himself.

"Just a few knocks from my last sail."

"That where you got those bruises on your arms?"

"Yeah, I got tossed around pretty good."

They stood there for the longest time, just inches apart, and Tess traced her route across the Pacific. She could feel his breath on her neck as she pointed to distant stops like the Marquesas, Tuamotu Islands, Tonga, and Fiji. Then he brushed against her for a closer look as she limned the course over the top of Australia, across the Indian Ocean to Durban, around the Cape of Good Hope into the South Atlantic, where the winds would push her home.

"That's a long way by yourself," he said. "Don't think I'd be brave enough to do it."

"You're just smarter than I am."

They were side by side, staring at the whole wide world that she was going to circle. She rubbed one of her bruises, then turned to Charlie and looked into his caramel eyes. "Where do you dream of going, Chas?" She heard herself call him by a nickname—it just came out, but she liked the sound of it.

"Zanzibar, Tasmania, the Galapagos. Everywhere . . ."

"So why don't you?"

He pushed his hands into his pockets and sighed. "Too many responsibilities here."

"All work and no play?"

He didn't answer. For the first time this evening, there was a twinge of discomfort. Despite his smile and twinkle, this man was hiding something. Then, up from deep inside her, came a reaction so surprising that she felt giddy. Instead of wanting to run from his secrets, she just wanted to be closer.

"Come on," she said, "what's stopping you?"

His eyes dodged her and then he flashed that smile that must have gotten him out of most tight spots. "Let's take a walk."

"In the cemetery? It's the middle of the night."

"Anybody who'd sail solo around the world can't be scared of a cemetery."

She wasn't so sure.

"C'mon," he said, grabbing her button-down and two coats. "I want to show you something."

SIXTEEN

IT WAS MIDNIGHT IN WATERSIDE, AND THICK FOG OOZED between the monuments. The moon was invisible behind the clouds, great walls of darkness closed in on every side, and Charlie led the way across the lawn. All was silent, and even their footfalls were muffled by the murk. Marble angels and granite nymphs appeared from nowhere as his flashlight slashed the gloom.

It was the witching hour, and Charlie was under a spell. Everything about Tess had thrown him off balance in the best possible way. Sure, his nervousness had made him go on too long about the origins of the St. Cloud family name in Minnesota. Yes, he had filibustered about the differences between cirrus and stratus accumulations. And yet, he could tell she was having fun. She was knocking back beers and laughing at his jokes.

From the moment she had come strolling down West Shore Drive at 8:00 P.M. sharp, he had tried to memorize every detail about the evening. Her hair was blowing wild, and when he greeted her with an outstretched hand, she ignored it, got up on her tiptoes, and kissed him hello on the cheek.

"Dinner ready?" she said. "I'm starving."

Sure enough, she ate two portions of everything and was lavish with her praise of the food. He loved the way she seemed to devour life, savoring every bite. He told real stories, not the canned ones that usually came out on dates. Tonight he had dispensed with the usual version that he projected to the world: the young man content with his job in the cemetery, the happy-go-lucky guy who never wanted to leave Marblehead. Tess drew out the real Charlie, the one with dreams of breaking free of everything and everyone that reined him in.

He even wanted to tell her about his maps on the wall, the sunset tables, and how those concentric circles governed his life. The rings on the charts showed the ambit of his world, demarcating exactly how far he could go from Waterside and still get back for Sam. A trip to Cape Cod. A drive up to New Hampshire. The outer circle was the absolute farthest he could go. Beyond that line, there was no chance of making it home in time. The promise would be broken and his brother would be gone. It could be dangerous sharing all this with Tess, but now, with the night winding down, he was feeling safer and ready to reveal a little more.

"First you get me drunk, then you take me on a forced march," she was saying as they tramped up a hill. "Where are we going?"

"Trust me, it's special."

They walked on, and the moon finally poked through the clouds, gently touching headstones in every direction. "We used to sneak in here all the time when we were kids," Tess said. "I made out with my first boy behind that obelisk over there."

"Who was the lucky guy?"

"Tad Baylor. I think he was in your class."

"The human fly?" Tad had run afoul of the law junior year, when he was captured stealing final exams from the copy room after scaling the wall of the administration building and climbing through a fourth-floor window. "You have excellent taste."

"I was fourteen," she said, "and he was a great kisser."

They kept on going across the lawns. An owl hooted from the treetops. The air was cool, and Charlie buttoned up his pea coat.

"So how long have you worked here?" Tess asked as they passed through a plot of Revolutionary War graves.

"Thirteen years," Charlie said. "Barnaby Sweetland gave me my first job here when I was in high school. He was the caretaker for thirty years. Remember him? The guy had a voice like an angel, and he ran the chorus at the Old North Church. Every day in the field, planting, cutting, sweeping, we could hear him singing to the skies."

Charlie kneeled down near a gravestone and pointed his flashlight at the damp ground. "Barnaby showed me every single thing I know about this place." He scooped up a handful of damp earth with an unmistakable aroma. "You've probably smelled this your whole life when you've gone outside in the rain. It comes from these strange compounds called geosmins. Barnaby taught me the chemical names for everything."

Tess started to laugh. "Be still my heart," she said.

Charlie smiled. His mind was cluttered with all sorts of obscure information, but now he had to wonder: Would a girl setting off to conquer the world ever really fall for a guy who lived in a cemetery and knew why grass and dirt smelled the way they did?

"This way," he said, pushing forward into the night.

"So whatever happened to Barnaby?" Tess said, following closely.

"One winter he took a long walk in a snowstorm and never came back. I found his body up there on the Mount of Memory." Charlie aimed the flashlight into the night. "He had a choir book with a note in it, saying he was tired of working so darn hard. After seventy-two years on earth, he was ready for the next world."

"You mean he killed himself?"

"I don't think so. He just wanted to spend the rest of eternity singing. That's where he promised I would always be able to find him. You know, in the songs of the choir and the organ on Sundays."

"Was he right? Can you still hear him?"

"Yes," Charlie said. "If I pay attention, he's always there in the music."

They had reached the crest of a hill where two willows hovered over a small, square stone building above the harbor. Guarding the entrance were two columns and a pair of crossed baseball bats. Tess walked straight to the front steps. Charlie aimed the flashlight at the name St. Cloud carved on the lintel.

"Your brother," she said.

"Yes, Sam." Charlie traced the sharp outline of the structure with his beam. "Mausoleum, noun," he said. "A floor covering used in crypts." He paused. "That's one of Sam's jokes."

Tess smiled, touching the smooth stone. "Is it all marble?"

"Imported from Carrara. They spared no expense. The driver of the eighteen-wheeler that hit us was drunk out of his mind. His company paid for every inch of this. It was all about public relations." He ran the flashlight down one of the columns. "They gave the guy five years, but he got away with three for good behavior. He's probably in a bar right now getting loaded."

"I'm so sorry."

"Don't be." He shook his head. "It was my fault. I never should've taken Sam to Fenway, and we never should've been on the bridge in the first place. If I'd been paying any attention, I could've avoided the crash, you know, gotten out of the way of the truck."

And so without noticing, Charlie broke one of his cardinal rules. He began talking about Sam. With everyone else in the world, he had always dodged the topic. It only made folks uncomfortable and awkward. But, he could tell, Tess was different. From the moment he met her, he knew she would understand.

He sat down on the steps of the mausoleum and said, "You were right this afternoon. Sam is why I work here. I promised I'd always take care of him."

"So you think he's around?"

Charlie looked up at her. "As sure as I am of anything."

"God, if only I had that same certainty about my father." She sat down beside him. He could smell her shampoo and feel her warmth. "I wish I knew Dad was close by."

"What makes you think he isn't?" Charlie said.

"There'd be some kind of sign, don't you think?"

"I think those signs are all around if you know where to look."

He made an absentminded looping motion with the flashlight beam, and as it swept the darkness he saw the most unexpected sight: Sam was hanging upside down from a hemlock branch and making a funny face. Charlie shut off the beam and leaped to his feet.

"What's wrong?" Tess said.

"Nothing. Just got a chill." He flipped the flashlight on again, turned it in the direction of the branch, but Sam was gone.

"You were telling me about Sam," she said. He focused on her emerald eyes. Did she really want to hear the answers? He was about to speak, but with his peripheral vision he saw something move. Over her shoulder in the light of the emerging moon, there was Sam racing across the lawn with Oscar.

"What do you miss most about him?" Tess asked.

"I miss punching him in the nose when he was a brat," he said in a voice that he hoped Sam would hear. "He liked to spy on people even when it was totally inappropriate." Charlie checked over Tess's shoulder again, and now Sam was gone.

"Most of all," he continued, "I miss that feeling when you go to sleep at night and when you wake up in the morning. It's the feeling that everything is all right in the world. You know, that amazing feeling that you're whole, that you've got everything you want, that you aren't missing anything. Sometimes when I wake up, I get it just for a moment. It lasts a few seconds, but then

I remember what happened, and how nothing has been the same since."

"You think that'll ever go away?"

"I doubt it." And then, incredibly, he found himself opening up even more. "Some days are better than others. You know, I finish work and hang out at the Barnacle or shoot pool at Bay State Billiards. It feels like it's gone, and I'm just like everyone else. Then, without warning, it comes back and lodges in my mind. That's when I don't feel right being around anyone. So I stay here behind the gates, listening to music, thinking, and reading books. I guess I never really know when it'll hit me. It's like the weather. Blue sky one day, thunder and rain the next."

"Same for me," she said, her voice almost a whisper. "But it's strange. Tonight's the first time in two years that I haven't missed him so much it hurts." Then she smiled and did the most incredible thing. She reached over and squeezed his hand.

A hemlock branch snapped behind Tess. She spun around, surprised by the noise. A fistful of needles landed on her shoulder. She turned to Charlie with one eyebrow arched. "Did you just see something? What was that?!"

He laughed. "You wouldn't believe me if I told you."

"Go ahead, try me."

"Maybe it was your dad."

Tess scoffed. "If Dad was here, he wouldn't pussyfoot around making tree branches snap. He'd really let me know." She stood up. "Tell the truth, do you really believe in that stuff?"

"Absolutely. I've seen too many things that defy explanation."

She chuckled. "You mean like twigs falling from a tree?"

"No," he said. "Like meeting you. Like dinner tonight."

She looked at him for a long moment. Her eyes seemed full of feeling. Then she abruptly changed the subject. "Charlie, tell me. You ever seen a ghost?"

Sam was now perched behind her on the roof of the mausoleum. His fingers were jammed into each corner of his mouth, stretching it wide into a funny face. Irritated, Charlie knew there was no good answer. He had gone far enough tonight and they were entering uncertain terrain. He didn't want to lie, but he didn't want to scare her away either, so he chose the safest route. "I've heard the Screeching Woman down by Lovis Cove."

"No way, the one killed by pirates?"

"The very one."

"So you think your brother and my father are here somewhere?"

"Maybe." Charlie looked for Sam in the darkness, and he popped up behind a gravestone. "But I don't think spirits stay here for very long unless they want to," he said. "I bet your dad has moved on to a better place."

"You mean heaven?"

"Sure, heaven. Or someplace else. Wherever it is, death isn't the end. It's an elevation, really. It's like catching the moon."

"Catching the moon?"

"It's hard to explain," he said. "I read somewhere that 75 billion human beings have lived and died since the beginning of history, and I believe their souls are out there somewhere." He looked straight up into the sky. "It makes me think of that John Lennon song. You know, 'We all shine on in the moon and the stars and the sun.'"

Tess was quiet for a long time. She stared into the opening between the clouds. The Milky Way spread out in a great swath. "I like that, Charlie," she said. "More than anything, I need to know he's out there somewhere. You know? That he's okay."

"He is," Charlie said. "Trust me. It's hard to explain, but I'm sure."

"You've got a feeling?"

He smiled. "Yeah, a feeling."

Then she turned to Charlie and said, "I'm glad you took me here tonight. It really means a lot."

"Me too."

They were so close together now that Charlie thought he could actually feel an electrical charge. He had heard touchy-feely types talk about energy fields before, and it seemed like hooey, but Tess definitely had one. He leaned forward the tiniest amount, watching for her reaction, hoping she would give him an opening. They stayed there in each other's glow for what felt like forever, until she looked down at her watch and said, "I better go."

For a moment, Charlie felt defeated, but then he decided to be daring. She was leaving in a few days, and who knew if he would see her again. So without saying a word, he reached for her waist and pulled her close. To his surprise, she came to him without resistance. She tilted her head back and her lips parted. He kissed her softly and tumbled into the most incredible feeling. It lasted only a few seconds, but it was bliss. The warmth reached all the way inside and filled him with the most exhilarating sensation he had ever known.

"Tad Baylor, eat your heart out," she said when they pulled apart. Then she grabbed his flashlight, twirled around, and marched off toward the great iron gates.

*   *   *

The streets were almost entirely deserted as Tess hurried past Five Corners and the Rip Tide Lounge, a fancy name for the rough dive where she had waitressed on breaks from college. Across the street, she saw a burly man staggering down the sidewalk. He was carrying a mug of beer and was trying unsuccessfully to keep it from sloshing. Tess slowed down. It was Minty Weeks, a retired fisherman and one of the better drinkers around. He had earned his nickname back in the great freeze of '79 when he was spotted ice-skating half-naked on the frozen harbor with a bottle of peppermint schnapps in each hand. An editorial in *The Marblehead Messenger* had called it the most scandalous display of public nudity since the actress Tallulah Bankhead had run through town with no clothes on and was locked up in the BB-gun closet at the police station because there was no jail for women.

"Hey, Minty," she called out. "Need any help getting home?"

He grunted, turned away from her, and faced a brick wall. He leaned his forehead against the building, fumbled with his zipper, and began to relieve himself.

She shook her head at this fine Marblehead specimen. "Have a good one," she said. She walked up Washington and Middle Streets, past Abbot Hall, where the clock on the tower gonged one, then turned on Lookout Court. She jumped the three steps up to her green colonial in a single bound and let herself in the unlocked front door. It was the kind of community where neighbors looked out for each other and no one ever used a dead bolt or key.

"Hey, Bobo!" she said. "Where are you, boy?" She had forgotten to leave a light on and was surprised her retriever wasn't waiting at the door for her to return. "Bobo?!"

She flipped on the lamp in the living room and saw her dog on the big couch. He was lying with his head on a pillow and was staring right at her, but he didn't move an inch.

"What? No love for your girl?" she said. "I bet you're hungry."

She went into the kitchen, switched on another light, and found a note from Tink by the toaster.

Hey, Girl,

    Took Bobo out & ate your leftovers. I was tempted to try on your clothes, but not my size. Too bad. See you mañana at your mom's dinner.

                     Love,

                     Me

ps—I'm doing yoga tonight with La Channing! Check in when you're back . . . make sure I'm still alive.

She chuckled. Tink hadn't seen his toes in years. It was too late to call, so she got out some Eukanuba, scooped the food into Bobo's bowl, and set it on the floor. "C'mon, boy. Chow time." Bobo was twelve years old and a little hard of hearing, but he still had some bark in him. A special present from Dad, he was waiting in a wicker basket on the front porch when she got home from her very first day of high school. Guys would come and go and maybe even break her heart, but Bobo was always true.

She went back into the living room. "Hey, what's the matter, boy?" The dog shook his head, let out a sleepy woof, and buried his nose in his paws. "Okay, I'll take you on a big run tomorrow, all the way to the lighthouse. And I'll make you scrambled eggs and bacon for breakfast. How's that?" He snorted.

Tess saw the light flashing on her answering machine. One message. She walked over and hit play. She heard her mother's voice: "Tessie, it's me. Just a reminder. Dinner at six tomorrow. If you're back earlier and feel like brunch with the old ladies, swing by church in the morning. It would be nice for everyone to see you before you go." There was a pause. Then she said, "Love you."

Tess climbed the slanting stairs to the second floor. "C'mon, boy," Tess said. "Bedtime for Bobo." She turned on the television and switched to the Weather Channel. A reporter was finishing a story about the damage from that nasty storm. It had slammed a bunch of tuna boats returning to Gloucester, sunk a tug somewhere near Providence, and was moving down to Delaware and Maryland. "Yeah, and it almost killed me," she said, shaking her head.

She slipped off her shirt and jeans, took off her bra, and changed into her tattered #11 Drew Bledsoe football jersey and some thick wool socks.

She hopped onto the four-poster bed, threw her head back on the pillows, and knew she was never going to get to sleep. She felt wired, like she could fly. It was Charlie St. Cloud and that incredible kiss. Damn, it was too short. She should have stayed a little longer and given him a little more of a test drive, but she knew that was dangerous. She didn't entirely trust herself in those situations. She easily could have followed him back to that cottage and spent the night. Of course, she wouldn't have necessarily slept with him. She wasn't that kind of girl. But she might have done just about everything else.

So why had she run? It was an old habit born of experience and disappointment. She couldn't remember exactly when, but somewhere along the way, she had given up even imagining that a guy could sweep her away. She had turned off those emotional faucets, and they were rusty from disuse. It was better that way. She once calculated that there had to be someone out there in a world of 6.3 billion people who would love her well and long. She even planned to sail out to find him. It was a romantic idea, but deep down, she knew the truth. She would spend four months all alone on the water, never docking long enough to get attached.

She got out of bed, pulled on her big red bathrobe, and stepped into the hall. Then she climbed the steep ladder up to the widow's walk on top of the house. It was a small square room enclosed in glass that looked on the harbor below and the twinkling lights of Boston to the southwest. For hundreds of years, women had climbed these rungs to watch their men return from the sea. Tess laughed: She loved turning tradition on its head. Soon, her family and friends would climb this ladder to look for her mast when she was on her way back from the other side of the world.

She lit the candles on the window ledge. Then she curled up on a banquette and pulled a blanket around her. She leaned her head against the cold glass and watched her breath on the pane. There was Waterside in the distance. For the first time, she noticed a little light in the black patch of woods. It was surely

Charlie's cottage. What a strange and magical place, surrounded by sad reminders of his loss, and yet so warm and safe with all those books, maps, music, and food.

She fought the feeling as long as she could, but then she pictured his hands on her waist, pulling her toward him, and the exhilaration of pushing up against his body. She wanted to kiss him again, and she was half tempted to go back downstairs, get on her bike, dash across town, ring that buzzer, and jump him right there at the gates. Then she had an even better idea and closed her eyes to imagine the possibilities. First light was just hours away, and she could hardly wait. Tomorrow would be an unforgettable day.

SEVENTEEN

CHARLIE SAT ON THE DOCK IN THE WATERSIDE COVE, leaned against one of the old wood posts, and sipped his morning coffee. He was still sleepy from staying up so late replaying every detail of the evening and hoping Tess was doing the same. Well past midnight, he had escorted her to the great iron gates and reluctantly let her go.

"You sure you don't want me to walk you home," he had said, hoping for another kiss or two.

"That's okay," she said.

"What about all the ghosts and goblins in the streets?"

"I'm a big girl, and no one's dumb enough to mess with me."

Then she had taken off into the night.

When he had gotten back to the cottage, his head

was still spinning, his lips still tingling, so instead of cleaning up, he had kicked back with another beer and the blue-eyed soul of Dusty Springfield and surrendered to the incredible feeling inside, like frozen ground beginning to thaw. The surface looked the same, but everything underneath was changing.

Now, as wriggles of steam rose from his mug to vanish in the bluish gray of the morning, he listened to the boom of the cannons at the yacht clubs across the water signaling the official arrival of the sun. This was how most days began in Marblehead. Coffee on the dock. A few captains motoring by with the latest on where the water was sharky and where the stripers were hitting. A chat with a WWII old-timer about the achy, arthritic northeast wind.

Then work.

But Sundays were different. There was no official business in the cemetery, so Charlie could take his time. The gates opened to the community at 8:00 A.M., but there were no burials. Joe would come by soon in the *Horny Toad*, and they would shoot across the harbor to the Driftwood for breakfast. Then they would hang out with the wharf rats who were burning off the hours till the NFL began.

"Heads up!" a voice cried out. Charlie turned just in time to see a tennis ball fly by his head with Oscar chasing at full speed.

"Morning, big bro," Sam said, stepping from the mist onto the dock. He was wearing a gray sweatshirt with its hood pulled up over his head. Messy curls drooped over his eyes. Even though playing catch at sunset was the key to renewing their promise, sometimes Sam dropped by at daybreak before taking off on his adventures.

"Morning," Charlie said.

"Soooooo?" Sam said, plopping down beside his brother.

"So what?"

"Don't play dumb! How was the action last night?" Oscar had captured the ball and was back, wagging his tail, ready for more.

"None of your business," Charlie said, hurling the ball onto the rocky shore. "If you weren't dead, I'd beat your brains in for spying."

"Gimme a break. I followed the rules. I kept my distance."

"You were pushing it. You were right up against the line, and you know the code." When folks had begun whispering that Charlie was losing his mind and talking to the ghost of his brother, Sam had agreed he wouldn't interfere when others were around. Still there were times when he couldn't resist making trouble.

"I like her," Sam said. "She's okay, even though she roots for the Pats."

Charlie didn't answer.

"Look at you, playing Mr. Cool. So what happened?"

"Nothing."

"Why'd she take off so fast last night? You kissed her, then she split. Bite her tongue or something?"

"It was getting late, I guess. It was only our first date."

"You think she got spooked by the cemetery?"

"No, she doesn't scare easily."

"Maybe you bored her to death with all your usual stuff about clouds."

"Very funny."

Sam poked at one of the nails in a post. Oscar brought the ball back and sat down for a rest, his tail thumping the boards. "What's a real kiss feel like?" Sam asked. He plopped down on the dock next to his beagle. "You know, a kiss with all the works."

"All the works?" Charlie smiled at his kid brother. Even though all those years had gone by since the accident, Sam remained twelve years old, forever asking innocent questions about the things in life that he would never know. He could have moved on to the next level and opened himself up to all the wisdom and enlightenment in the universe, but he chose to stay.

"There's nothing like it," Charlie said, "and there are a zillion different kinds. Some are exciting and sexy and—"

"Slippery?"

"I can't do this."

"C'mon. I wanna know!"

Charlie had to think. A kiss? How do you explain a kiss? "Remember that Little League game when you played the Giants?"

"Yup."

"Tell me the story."

Sam grinned. "We were down four to one in the last inning. I came to the plate with two outs, the bases loaded, and Gizzy Graves was on the mound. I missed the first two pitches by about a mile. The shortstop started laughing at me, but I smashed the next pitch over the left-field fence for a home run."

"And how'd it feel?"

"Best thing in the world."

"That's a kiss, minus the bat."

Sam laughed. "And minus Gizzy Graves."

"Exactly."

Charlie watched his little brother and felt the hurt. In the abstract, Sam understood the concept of the perfect kiss, but actually experiencing one was entirely different. Charlie was suddenly swept up in all the amazing things Sam was going to miss. He had been cheated of so much.

And then Charlie noticed an older woman coming down the hill from the cemetery, picking her way between the tombstones. It was Mrs. Phipps, and Charlie could see that she was already beginning to fade away. Sometimes it happened quickly; other times it took a few days or weeks. Folks seemed to move on when they were ready. The soft morning light was glinting right through her. Gone were the black dress, stockings, and pointy shoes. Now she was wearing a pink frock with a matching pillbox hat and silver boots. The lines in her face had softened. Her skin was smooth, and her hair was darker. She seemed neither young nor old but a perfect balance of the two. Charlie recognized the transformation. This was the way Mrs. Phipps wanted to see herself. It was a shimmering reflection of the past and present as well as a projection of the future. It was the combination of who she had once been and who she always hoped to be. It was always this way when folks crossed over.

"Good morning," she said, stepping onto the dock.

"You're looking lovely, Mrs. Phipps," Charlie said. "How are you feeling?"

"Much better. I guess the shock has worn off, just like you said it would."

Charlie motioned to his brother to stand up out of respect. "Mrs. Phipps, this is my brother, Sam."

"How do you do?"

"Hi," Sam said. "Nice hat."

She tilted her head. "I wore this on the day my sweet Walter asked me to marry him." She was smiling. "You know, I just hated that old black dress they stuck me in at the funeral home. Don't know why my daughter picked it out of the closet. It's hardly how I want to look when I see my husband again."

Charlie knew she was ready, and sure enough she said, "I just wanted to stop by and say farewell. It's time for me to go. He's waiting for me." She reached out with her shimmering hand. "Good-bye and thank you."

"Good luck," Charlie said.

"Bye," Sam added.

Mrs. Phipps walked away and was almost transparent by the time she reached the end of the dock. Then a horn hooted on the water. Joe was steering his boat into the cove.

"Ahoy," he said. He was wearing a Bruins cap turned backward, a red checked shirt, and jeans. "Top of the morning to you."

Charlie waved, then mumbled to his little brother, "Gotta go."

"See you at sundown," Sam said, scooping up Oscar.

Charlie jumped onto the boat, and Joe pushed forward on the throttle. He aimed for the wharf across the harbor. "Look at you!" Joe said. "You're all happy today."

"What're you talking about?"

"You've got a bounce in your step. A grin on your face. Tell the truth. You get laid last night?"

"No comment."

"You snake! What's her name?" He spun the steering wheel hard, narrowly avoiding a moored catamaran.

Charlie leaned into the wind and shook his head. He zipped

the front of his navy fleece. Tess was his secret, and he was going to hold on to it as long as he could. The last thing he needed was Joe meddling or making a play for her himself. "Nice day, huh?"

"Nice day, schmice day. Come on, Chucky Love! Tell me everything. Who is she? Where did you meet her?"

"You over or under on the Pats today?" Charlie said.

"The truth will come out," Joe said, idling the engine and letting the boat drift toward the wharf. The dock was already crowded with other vessels, and he deftly steered into an open slot. Charlie climbed out, tied up, and headed for the Driftwood, a small wood-frame shack with peeling red paint. Joe caught up with him, and the two stepped through the screen door.

Most of the little tables were already crowded with townies. Fish netting and harpoons dangled from the ceiling. A lacquered sand shark grimaced from one wall at a barracuda over the kitchen door, and Charlie still smiled at the urn above the cash register with a gold plaque that said: ASHES OF PROBLEM CUS-TOMERS.

Hoddy Snow, the harbormaster, was huddled in the back by the jukebox with his two deputies. Tink and a crew of sailors sat at their regular table in the front. Charlie approached Bony and his gang, took an empty seat, and asked, "What's going on?"

"Big news in the police blotter," one of the guys said. "Check this out. 'Midnight. Friday. A moan was heard from a bush on Rose Avenue. One squad car responded. Investigation turned up nothing.' "

"I bet it was Bony and his girlfriend," Charlie laughed.

"I wish," Bony said, "but if you ever hear me moaning in the bushes, you better call an ambulance."

Charlie saw Hoddy stand up in the corner. "Can I have your attention, fellas?" he said in an urgent voice. He was a hulking man, and his shiny Grecian Formula hair was combed neatly in law-enforcement style. He wore a snug polo shirt with his name and title sewn in block letters over his heart. "Your attention please." The room fell silent. "Sorry to interrupt your breakfast, but we've got a serious situation and we need everyone's help."

Hoddy definitely had a way with drama. A few years ago, he had appeared in an episode of *Unsolved Mysteries* to talk about the notorious fifty-four-year-old Atherton murder. And when Tucker Goodwin pulled up a dead body snagged in a lobster trap not long ago, Hoddy had a field day with the Boston papers and TV stations.

"It's a real bad situation," he was saying.

"Someone skinny-dipping in the harbor without a license?" Bony said.

"Knock it off," Hoddy said. "We just got a call from the Coast Guard in Gloucester. They want our help putting together a search. A fisherman picked up a life ring and a rudder floating off Halibut Point. They think it's from Marblehead."

"What boat?" Charlie said. "Whose is it?"

Hoddy's eyes narrowed. His voice choked up for a moment, and there was no doubting his seriousness. "It's *Querencia*," he said. "Tess Carroll's boat is missing."

EIGHTEEN

BOBO GALLOPED, LIKE A DOG POSSESSED, DOWN DEV-
ereux Beach.

Tess stood on the cool sand and called out to him
but he ignored her, charging ahead, splashing through
the surf. From the moment she had opened the door
at dawn, he had bolted into the street and taken off
without her. He was old, deaf, and arthritic, but they
still ran together every Sunday morning, cutting
through the quiet streets of the old town, loping along
the shore, looping around the Neck, and always finishing in the cemetery. Normally, he stayed on the leash,
lumbering along beside her, barking at the Blaneys'
cats on Merritt Street and nosing around the trash
cans behind the Shipyard Galley. But not today. He was
in some kind of hurry.

Tess felt the wind rising off the ocean as she

watched Bobo bound up to a fisherman sitting on a lawn chair. He was about 500 feet away, but she could tell it was Dubby Bartlett with his prized casting poles planted in the sand, lines spinning out into the surf. He always fished there Sunday mornings while his wife was in church praying for them both.

"Dubby!" she called out. "Hold on to Bobo! I need to get him on the leash." He petted the dog, then looked up and down the shore, like he was expecting her to be right behind.

"Dubby!" she shouted again. "Over here!"

The wind was blowing pretty hard, sending up a spray of sand, and Tess's voice must have gotten lost in the swirl. Bobo jumped up on him, nuzzled his face, barked, then took off again. For a moment, Dubby watched the dog go, then he went back to his reels.

Tess gave chase again, shouting for the retriever to stop. She was getting angrier. What on earth had gotten into him? He was like a puppy again, totally uncontrollable, prancing along the shore, covering another mile without stopping.

"Bobo!" she yelled. "Come back here right now!" But the dog trotted along the trail that ended on the rocky banks of Waterside cove and ran up the sloping embankment through the back gates of the cemetery.

Tess lost sight of him but knew he was heading to the top of the hill speckled with tombstones. Strolling now between rows of markers, she saw Midge Sumner across the lawn. She was one of her mom's dear friends, bundled in her old purple parka, standing on a stepladder, cleaning the life-size statue of her sister Madge, who'd died of pneumonia as a child. Midge came every weekend to wash Madge's plaster ears with Q-tips and scrub her body with sandalwood soap.

Midge was too busy scouring to notice her, so Tess kept heading toward her dad's grave, where she knew Bobo would be sitting by the headstone.

"You're a bad dog!" she said. "What the heck has gotten into you?" Bobo rolled over and scratched his back in the grass. "Don't think you can charm your way out of this," she said. "I'm really mad. That was crazy!" She sat down beside him and ignored his yelps.

Instead, she looked out on the harbor and was amazed by the strange brilliance of the day. The blue of the ocean seemed more vivid than ever, and the sails on the boats shone like mirrors against the sun. *Querencia*'s mooring was blocked by a gorgeous Dijkstra forty-two-meter schooner that had probably come into the harbor to pick up gear from Doyle Sails. Tess inhaled the unmistakable odor of herring bait from the lobster traps stacked on the wharf. Even her sense of smell was more acute today, and the fishy fragrance reminded her of Dad coming home every night from the sea. Then she heard laughter and shouting behind her. She turned and saw a beagle sprint from the woods, chased by a gangly boy in jeans and a gray sweatshirt.

"I'm going to get you!" the kid was yelling, his Red Sox cap askew on the dark curls spilling from its brim.

Tess stood up and called out, "Hey! You need a hand?"

The boy saw her and stopped running. A puzzled expression crossed his freckled face, and he approached slowly. His beagle was growling at Bobo, and the kid asked softly, "Does he bite?"

"No," she said. "He's an old guy. Lost most of his teeth."

The kid dropped his mitt, kneeled down, and gave the retriever a big scratch on the belly. Then he looked up at Tess with curious eyes.

"He likes that," she said. But the boy didn't answer. He just stared.

"What?" she said.

"Nothing."

"Nothing? Nobody looks at someone like you're looking at me and it's nothing."

"You can see me?"

"Of course I can."

"But that's impossible."

Tess assumed the kid was playing a game. "Are you invisible or something?"

"Yes."

"Wow. That's pretty cool. What's your secret?"

Sam didn't answer. The boy and his beagle just stared. It was beginning to unnerve her a little. Then, after a long moment, he finally said, "What's your story? When did you get here?"

"Just a few minutes ago," Tess said. "My dad's buried here. So are my grandparents and great-grandparents."

"That makes sense," Sam said, picking up his glove and ball. "You feeling all right?"

"Definitely," Tess said. "Hey, you play for Marblehead?"

"Obviously not anymore." There was an awkward silence. Then he said, "You're Tess, right?"

"How'd you know?"

"I heard about you."

"Really?"

"Yeah, from Charlie," he said. Oscar barked at the sound of his name.

"Charlie?"

"He'd kill me for saying anything. Swear you won't tell."

"Cross my heart." She smiled.

"He hasn't sucked face with anyone in a really long time," Sam said. "I think he likes you."

Tess felt a twinge of embarrassment. "Well, I like him too." Her cheeks felt warm from blushing. "You know where I can find him right now? Is he home?"

"Did he know you were coming?"

"No. I didn't tell him."

"What else didn't you tell him?" Sam said. His eyes were locked on.

"I'm not quite sure what you mean." The kid was starting to get to her again. *It's those video games,* she thought. *It'll ruin them all.* "Do me a favor, okay? Give Charlie a message?"

"Sure."

"Let him know I came by."

"Will do."

The kid threw his ball and the beagle took off after it. "Hey, Tess," he said. "You play catch?"

"Sure."

"You throw like a girl?"

"Not on your life."

"Then come back tonight. Charlie's always here at sundown. See that forest over there? The big blue spruce?"

"Yes."

"Follow the trail on the other side of the old log."

"And then what?"

"You'll find us in the clearing. We'll throw the ball around."

"Sounds fun," she said. "I'll see you later." She took a few steps down the hill. She was liking the thought of playing catch with Charlie and the boy. Then she spun around, and said, "Hey, kid, what's your name?"

He hesitated for an instant before he answered. "I'm Sam. Sam St. Cloud."

III

IN BETWEEN

NINETEEN

THE OCEAN HAD NEVER LOOKED SO MASSIVE. WHITECAPS
streaked to the horizon, and the thirty-five-foot Down
East lobster boat careened through the waves. With
one hand, Charlie steadied himself on the dashboard;
with the other, he peered through binoculars and
swept the confused seas. He and Tink were running a
track leg in a search pattern on Jeffreys Ledge, an area
not too far from where the fisherman had picked up
debris from *Querencia*.

That morning in the Driftwood, he had absolutely
refused to believe the news about Tess. At first, he had
erupted: "No way. It's not possible." Then all eyes in
the restaurant had focused on him.

"You know something we don't?" Hoddy had
asked.

Charlie had wanted to tell them about her visit to

her father's grave and their dinner in the cottage. He had wanted to describe their midnight walk and even their first kiss. But he had suddenly felt afraid. It was an unconscious reflex. Maybe something terrible had happened to *Querencia* on the water, and it was Tess's spirit that had come to the cemetery. It wasn't impossible, and in that instant, he knew he had to protect himself. "She's got to be around somewhere," he had mumbled, trying to mask his confusion. "Don't you think?"

"What're you talking about?" Tink had said, stepping forward. "They found her rudder and a life ring. There's been no word from her in more than thirty-six hours. What more do you need?"

Charlie had felt himself scrambling. "What about her house? Anyone look there?"

"Of course," Hoddy had said. "No luck. Dubby Bartlett saw her dog running on the beach without a leash this morning. Her mother was expecting to hear from her by now, but there's been no word."

And so the men had paired off to start the search. Charlie joined up with Tink, who had borrowed a powerful lobster boat. The two had known each other only casually from the local beer-and-clam circuit, but they were both hell-bent on finding Tess.

In the early hours, the search had produced all sorts of junk, including a floating Coleman cooler with a few Buds and a Nike golf bag minus the clubs.

Then in the middle of the day, they had spotted a life raft that was partially inflated and blackened with smoke. Hauling it aboard, Tink unraveled when he realized it belonged to *Querencia*. First, he unleashed a gut-wrenching scream, then he shouted: "No!" That single, simple syllable stretched into an agonizing wail until he ran out of breath, and great gobs of tears coursed down his cheeks, soaking his scruffy beard.

The boat had vanished. Tess was nowhere.

The only life they witnessed all day on that angry ocean was a pod of humpback whales breaching two hundred yards to starboard, spray blasting from their blowholes before they dived to the depths.

In the outer reaches of his mind, Charlie began to wonder what had really happened. Was it Tess in the cemetery last night or her spirit? He had seen thousands of souls come and go and he knew all the vaporous clues. He had never before been fooled. They all gleamed with an aura of light. The old no longer hobbled. The infirm were restored with vigor. At first, their edges would soften and shimmer like gossamer. Then their appearance would change subtly, and they would begin to look the way they had always imagined themselves. Soon, when they were ready to go on to the next level, they would fade away, deliquescing like mist in the sun.

But Tess was different. He had gazed into her emerald eyes. He had stood right next to her. He had listened to her incredible laugh. He had even felt himself falling a little in love. No, she couldn't have been a spirit. There was nothing diaphanous about her. She was too real, too substantial, too alive. There had to be some mistake.

A wave crashed over the deck, slapping him hard across the face and stinging his eyes. He fought to keep them open, struggling not to blink, for fear of missing her in the water. All day he had prayed to God that He would not take away a person so fine and rare. For each disturbing fact, Charlie had supplied an optimistic answer. Her boat wasn't in its mooring where it belonged, but the ocean was vast and she could be sailing anywhere. That debris recovered by the fisherman wasn't necessarily proof of a shipwreck. Maybe it had just fallen off *Querencia*.

Still, there was the matter of the burned-out life raft. Charlie checked the digital gauges on the dashboard. The thermometer indicated the ocean was fifty-two degrees. From paramedic training he knew that cold water stole body heat thirty times faster than air. Without protective gear, unconsciousness would occur after thirty to sixty minutes and death in one to three hours. But even if her boat had burned and gone to the bottom, Tess had a survival suit onboard that was good for at least seventy-two hours in these temperatures. That was still plenty of time to find her.

In the western sky, Charlie saw splashes of rust and plum. The clouds were bunching in great gouts. The angle of the sun was low on the water, and he suddenly realized for the first time in thirteen years he hadn't thought about Sam all day. Not even once. Now his heart began to pound. He could feel the panic. There was only an hour of light left to find her—and an hour of light to get home. It was an impossible situation.

Tess was missing. Sam was waiting.

Just then, Tink turned the wheel sharply. "Tank's almost empty," he said. "We're losing the sun. I hate to go back to port, but we don't have much choice."

Charlie nodded but felt no relief. It would be incredibly close. "Want me to drive?" he asked, thinking he could increase their speed and improve his chances.

"I'm fine," Tink said.

So Charlie went to the stern and sat down. He put his head in his hands and closed his eyes. He saw Tess sashaying down the gravel walk in the cemetery. He imagined her pirouetting in the night. And then he replayed every moment in his mind, trying to make sense of it all.

Maybe her beauty had overwhelmed him. Maybe the sparks had distracted him from the signs. Or maybe God had some other reason. How could he have been so wrong?

Charlie stood and moved forward to the cockpit beside Tink. He glanced at the speedometer. Fifteen knots. Tink's face was flushed, and he was grazing through a giant bag of Oreos. There were black crumbs on his chin.

Charlie looked out and watched a shag dive for mackerel behind the boat. The low light of dusk was slanting off the water, and he knew the sun would be gone at 6:33 P.M.

"Can we speed up a bit?" he asked gently.

"What's your frigging problem, Mario Andretti? Why the big hurry?"

"I just need to get back."

He turned the wheel five degrees to starboard. "You got something more important to do? A hot date? League night at the Bowl-O-Mat?"

Charlie didn't even bother to answer. He stood silently, listening to the thud of the waves against the boat. After a while, Tink reached out with the Oreo bag. A peace offering.

"No, thanks."

"Look, I'm sorry. My nerves are fried." He rubbed his big hands on the wheel. Charlie thought he saw tears in the man's eyes. Then Tink said, "So how do you know Tess again?"

"We just met."

But Tink wasn't really listening. He seemed lost in his own fears. "I never should've let her go out into that storm," he said.

That was strange. Tess hadn't mentioned bad weather. "Whatever happens," Charlie said, "she's going to be okay."

Tink looked over with sad eyes. "You think?"

"You just have to believe."

And that was exactly what Charlie was forcing himself to do—believe Tess was okay. But, of course, with every passing moment, with every empty stretch of ocean, his growing fear was that she wasn't. He knew all about the middle ground between life and death and how spirits separated from their bodies. He had been there briefly himself, only to be shocked back to life. He had to accept the possibility that Tess's soul had come to the cemetery to find her father without realizing what had happened to her body. Folks often showed up bewildered by their own heart attacks or aneurysms. Sometimes they didn't even comprehend that life was over and had to spend a few days figuring things out. Others knew right away what had brought them down, and they screamed at God and the world from the moment they arrived. They were the ones who held on to family and friends as long as they could. And then there were the folks who had it the easiest of all, letting go quickly and moving right on to the next realm.

So where did that leave Tess? Could she be wandering the streets of Marblehead, totally unaware that she was a spirit? Or, worse, maybe she had already taken the next step, and he would never see her again.

Up ahead, Charlie saw the mouth of the harbor. The sky was dark gray, and the lighthouse flashed its familiar green beam. As they passed the Corinthian Yacht Club, Rick Vickery, the dockmaster, was getting ready to strike the colors and fire the sunset salute cannon.

Tink steered toward the wharf and glided in smoothly. Charlie jumped out. As he tied up, he heard the blast of the guns. "I've got to run," he said.

"You sure you're okay?" Tink asked. "You don't look so good."

"I'm fine. Call me later if you hear anything."

"Will do," Tink said.

With that, Charlie took off in a sprint. He knew he would be late. Five minutes, maybe even ten. He raced up State Street, cut through an alley, hopped a picket fence, and dashed across Mrs. Dupar's lawn. A dog in the window barked as he flew past. A delivery van screeched when he cut across Washington.

It was almost dark in Marblehead. Lights glimmered behind curtains. Smoke spiraled from chimneys. And Charlie ran as fast as he could...

For Sam. And for life itself.

TWENTY

HE HAD A STITCH IN HIS SIDE AND HIS LUNGS ACHED AS HE made the last turn down West Shore Drive. When his fists closed at last around the heavy wrought-iron bars of the gates, he rested his forehead for a moment against the cool metal. Then he wiggled the key in the lock, tried to turn the latch, and, for the first time ever, it wouldn't open. He felt a shot of panic, pulled the key out, jammed it back in again, and twisted it with all his strength. He heard the metal click, and he hurried inside. The main gravel path felt good underfoot, and the wind brought the scent of burning leaves.

He found the utility cart beside the Fountain of Youth and he aimed the little vehicle toward the Forest of Shadows. He steered along the bumpy trail and stopped under the low branches of the blue spruce.

He was in such a hurry this time that he didn't even bother to check over his shoulder.

Instead, he reached under the front seat and patted around until he found the glove holding the ball in its firm embrace. Then he leaped over the old rotting log and dashed through the woods, up a little hill to its crest, past a copse of maple trees, then down beside a waterfall and swirling pool. A sliver of gray graced the canopy of the cedar grove as he tore into the clearing with its perfect lawn, ninety feet long and wide. In the twilight, he could just make out that the pitcher's mound, rubber, and plate were empty.

"Sam!" he yelled. "Sammm?"

The seesaw and swings hanging from the thick arm of the sycamore were empty too.

"Sam?!"

But there was no answer. Charlie could feel the dread begin to rise—first in his stomach, then his chest. His head began to pound. It certainly didn't help that he was so tired. Fear flooded through him.

He knew he had to stop himself from thinking the absolute worst. So he crossed a few yards of grass and settled onto the slat of wood suspended by ropes. He leaned back, kicked at the hollow of dirt beneath his feet. For a moment, he could see the crescent of moon right above his toes and then he swooped back again.

"Sam!" he tried again. A covey of doves burst from their nests in the spruce trees and flew into the darkening slash of horizon. When the rustle of wing beats passed and the air was still again, Charlie called once more.

"Sammm..."

And then, as his voice trailed off, a little miracle happened. Charlie heard a sound—so faint at first that he wasn't sure it was anything more than his own imagination.

"Charlie!"

There was Sam in his Sox cap, shorts, and high tops, coming from the forest. Oscar pranced behind him.

"Where've you been?" Charlie said, jumping from the swing. "You scared me."

"I'm here. Relax, everything's okay." Sam smiled. "Want to play catch?"

"No, I need to talk about something."

Sam walked over to the picnic table and sat down. "What's going on?" he said. "How was your day?"

"Miserable," Charlie said.

"What happened?"

"It's Tess."

Sam's eyes were wide. "So you found out."

Charlie felt his stomach clench. What did Sam know? How did he know it? "Have you seen her?" Charlie asked. "Has she been here today?"

"She came looking for you."

"You saw her?"

"Yes, I saw her." His voice was soft, like he was cushioning the blow. "And she saw me."

Charlie felt himself deflate. There was no denying it anymore. In all his years in Waterside, he had never met a living person who could see his brother, or any other ghost for that matter. Salem was full of self-proclaimed witches who claimed they could speak to the dead, but Charlie had never seen any proof. Psychics and mediums stopped by at Waterside all the time with desperate clients in tow. But again, they never seemed to notice Sam frolicking with Oscar on the grass or the spirits of their loved ones reaching out in a gentle breeze or sending an autumn leaf sailing onto their shoulders.

"Why didn't you tell me last night?" Charlie asked.

"I didn't know. Honest. I didn't get a good look," Sam said. "Remember? You didn't want me anywhere near her."

"Does she know yet?" Charlie asked.

"I'm not sure."

"What do you mean you're not sure?"

"I think she's figuring it out."

"Is she fading already? Is she moving on?"

"I can't tell."

Charlie threw his head back and looked up into the darkness. All day he had hoped she was alive, but now he understood she was a spirit in the middle ground. Across the western sky, he saw the fuzzy patches of the Magellanic Clouds, each with 200 billion stars like the sun, and he suddenly felt insignificant and without hope.

Sam was sitting right next to him, but for the first time it wasn't enough. Charlie knew he wanted more. He needed more. He ran his hands through his hair and wondered if Sam knew what he was thinking.

"It's going to be okay, big bro," Sam said softly.

"How can you be sure?"

"Don't worry," Sam said. "She's coming here tonight."

TWENTY-ONE

WHAT HAD BEGUN AS MERELY THE STRANGEST DAY OF HER life had quickly morphed into the most frightening. It had started with that headache that refused to go away and it had ended in total despair back at her father's grave.

After meeting Sam St. Cloud in the cemetery, Tess had spent the day in a thick soup of confusion. The kid was Charlie's brother, but he was dead, killed thirteen years ago in that terrible car wreck. How was it possible to have a conversation with him? Maybe it was true what they said: Hang around a graveyard too long and you start to see ghosts. Was the boy an apparition? Or was she hallucinating?

On the other hand, maybe it wasn't Sam St. Cloud at all. Perhaps it was some punk playing a stupid trick.

More than ever, she knew she had to see Charlie again, and she would ask him about his brother.

As the sun had risen over Marblehead and the weekend sailors had made their way from the harbor, Tess walked Bobo back home to Lookout Court. No one greeted her on the street, not even her old friend Tabby Glass, who was jogging on the far sidewalk behind a stroller with her new baby girl.

"Want some chow?" Tess asked when they finally reached her house, but Bobo just plunked down on the front steps.

"All right, suit yourself," she had said. "I'm going down to check on *Querencia*."

She jogged down the steep public stairs that descended the hill from her little street. She strolled along the waterfront. The colors of the hulls and the sails seemed brighter. The smell of salt in the air was sharper. The fryer from the Driftwood was sending up more smoke than ever.

She walked along the dock, stopped suddenly at her mooring, and in that instant, she knew something was really wrong. *Querencia* wasn't there. Tink would never have taken her out without asking permission. She felt a little woozy, and her head seemed to spin. She kneeled down to get her balance, bracing herself with one hand on a weathered plank. She thought she might be sick, leaned over the ledge, and peered into the water below. She adjusted her eyes and she gasped.

Her reflection was missing.

Only the sky and the clouds looked back at her. There was no outline of her head or body against the blue. There was not even a shadow on the water. A sudden numbness overwhelmed her. Tess finally understood.

She wasn't there at all.

Her mind raced back over the puzzling events of the last day. Nana not seeing her in the rest home. Bobo paying no attention to her commands. Dubby Bartlett ignoring her on the beach. No one had acknowledged her because no one could see her.

No one except Charlie St. Cloud and his dead brother Sam.

What on earth was going on?

She leaped up and spun around. She grabbed her waist and then her hair. She rubbed her jeans. She rolled a button on her shirt between her fingers. Everything felt as normal as ever. And yet it wasn't.

She called out to the old guys under the tree—Bony, Chumm, Iggy, and Dipper—but they kept on chatting, and her soul filled with dread. Something terrible must have happened. She tried to remember the boat and the storm. She could see herself capsizing, then fighting her way onto the deck after *Querencia* righted herself. But then what? Had she made it back to port? Her memory was a fog. She groped around but could grasp nothing.

When did she die?

The question seemed impossible. Tess felt the terror and turmoil inside. She desperately needed an anchor. Then she realized she only had to do one thing: Find Charlie. If anyone could explain what was happening, he could. But what if something had changed, and now he couldn't see her, like everyone else? What if she had become invisible to him too?

Anxiously, she tried to spot Charlie in the huge cemetery, but he was nowhere to be found. Finally, Tess all but threw herself on her father's grave under the Japanese maple. If this was death, she thought, then Dad would come to be with her. Or maybe he would be waiting for her somewhere else. Where was she supposed to go? What was she to do? Was there an information desk somewhere? A bulletin board? She didn't have a clue.

Then she began to cry and didn't stop until she fell asleep, exhausted. She awoke, gasping with fear that she would never find Charlie. The sky was almost dark, and as she pulled herself up from the grass, she remembered Sam's instructions: Find the blue spruce in the forest and the trail on the other side of the old log. She shuddered. The woods were so creepy last night. Could she do it alone? To her surprise, the forest was peaceful and calm. She followed the path past the waterfall and pool, then threaded her way through the cypress grove. Suddenly, she heard voices up ahead and a beagle's yowl. When she came into the clearing, there was Charlie on a bench.

The very sight of him lifted her spirits. At least she could be certain that part of her life was real. She just wanted him to tell her it was all some big mistake. She wanted to kiss him and start up exactly where they had left off last night.

As she approached, she prayed Charlie would still be able to see her, and when he leaped up and smiled at her, she felt an incredible wave of relief. She wasn't alone anymore. She heard his deep voice: "Thank God you're here. I was so afraid you were never coming back."

She was impossibly beautiful. Her hair was tousled around her shoulders. Her eyes were full of feeling. Charlie stood up to hug her hello. He reached out with his arms but she stopped short by one foot.

"Where have you been?" she asked. "I was looking all over for you."

"Been looking for you too," he answered. "I take it you met my brother."

"Hi, Sam," she said. They were the two sweetest words ever. Charlie had never imagined he would hear a woman greet his brother that way.

"Hi," Sam said. "Shame you got here so late. It's too dark to play catch." He turned to Charlie. "She says she doesn't throw like a girl! You believe her?"

"Now's not the time," Charlie said. He looked at Tess. She was just standing there—as real as anyone he had ever known. There wasn't a single sign that she was fading away. And yet, in his brain he knew she was. He wondered how much she understood. He decided to start with a simple question. "How are you doing?"

"I was fine until I couldn't see my reflection in the water," she said. "Now I'm just confused. Tell me what's going on, Charlie."

She obviously didn't know what had happened, and he knew he would have to be the one to break the news.

"Come on," she said. "I'm a big girl. I can handle it." She was obviously trying to be brave, but her tremulous voice gave her away. He had seen this before as spirits passed through Waterside. He ached over what she was going through—the confusion, the fear, the sadness.

"I'm not sure where to start," Charlie said.

"How about the beginning?"

"All right," he said. "*Querencia* has been missing for forty-eight hours. The whole town is worried sick. The fleet went out to search."

"Missing for forty-eight hours?" She stomped the ground. "Damn, that's a long time. . . ."

"A fisherman found a piece of your hull off Halibut Point. Tink and I found your life raft in Sandy Bay."

"Where?"

"Sandy Bay, off Rockport."

"That's strange. I wasn't anywhere near Rockport. Must've been the wind and the current." She walked over to the swing and sat down on the wood plank.

"Do you remember what happened?" Sam asked.

"Not really," she said.

Charlie watched her carefully. He hadn't missed any obvious clues. There were no telltale signs. She wasn't fading at the edges. There was no heavenly glow around her. She just seemed like herself, radiant as ever. She kicked her legs in the air, and the swing began to sway.

"You've got to try to remember," Charlie said. "We need to know where you were when it happened."

Tess jumped down from the swing. "Look, I know exactly what happened. The storm was Force 10, and I spent the night upside down on the water. It was freezing. A damn bottle of salad dressing shattered in the galley. It stank up the whole joint. I can still smell it on me."

"Then what?"

"Next thing, I was at Dad's grave."

"Do you remember coming back to port?"

"Not exactly."

"Do you know how you got to the cemetery?"

"No, Chas. It's a blur."

"That's okay," he said. "Sometimes when it happens suddenly, you don't even realize what's going on. It takes time to sink in." He watched her carefully, weighing the impact of his words.

She seemed dazed at first, then she said, "Dear God, what's going to happen to me?"

"Everything will feel better soon," he said, his voice choking on the words, "and you'll realize you're going home where you belong."

"Home? What are you talking about? Home is on Lookout Court with Bobo. Home is with my mother and friends." There were tears in her emerald eyes now. She brushed them away and tried to force a smile, but it came off a little crooked. Then she said, "And I was even beginning to think home might be with you."

TWENTY-TWO

TESS WASN'T A SUPERSTITIOUS SAILOR. SHE NEVER CARED if her crew said "pig," a word most mariners dreaded because of an obscure belief that swine could somehow see the wind and mentioning them could whip up gales. She even dared to whistle while she worked—another taboo on the water—and she never hesitated to set sail on Fridays, which for centuries had portended disaster. She often stepped onto her boat with her left foot first, and she insisted that *Querencia* be painted blue, a color associated with tragedy at sea.

Now, incredibly, she wondered if it had been stupid to keep testing her luck. She had brought flowers aboard her boat, even though seamen insisted they be reserved for funerals. She had always looked back to port after sailing out, another violation of the code.

Yes, she had broken the rules a thousand times or more, and Tess couldn't help thinking: Maybe this was her fault.

Night was falling on the forest. The moon was up, the stars were out, and Tess sat with Charlie and Sam at the picnic table in the clearing. She was trying to hold herself together. Crazy, random thoughts were flooding her brain. She didn't want to unravel in front of them. But little by little, the reality of it all was locking into her consciousness.

Life was over.

As she felt the bump on her head, she began to have flashes of what had really happened the night of the storm. The images struck her in fragments. She didn't have the whole picture yet, but she could see the waves overtaking her and the world going black.

Deep down, she glimpsed what death meant. . . .

She would never race solo around the world.

She would never sail the Strait of Malacca or the Sulu Sea.

She would never see her name in the Hall of Fame in Providence.

She would never walk down the aisle of the Old North Church.

She would never honeymoon in Spain or run with the bulls in Pamplona or see the sunny, safe spot in the bullrings of Seville.

She would never feel the miracle of new life kicking inside her.

She would never teach her daughter how to hoist a mainsail or strike a luff curve.

Worst of all—and this was what distressed her more than anything—she would never know true and lasting love.

She tried to stop herself. She never even thought about a list like this yesterday or the day before, but now it went on and on. . . .

She would never again taste the roast beef at Mino's. She would never bundle up and play in the Powder Puff game on Thanksgiving. These were her rituals, the routines that made her feel alive and connected. Without them, where would she be?

Lost.

And there was this wonderful new man. She would never get to know this Charlie St. Cloud, who appeared from nowhere in her life and instantly was snatched out of reach. Why had she met him now? God must have had a reason.

She tried to concentrate on what Charlie and Sam were saying, taking turns describing the afterlife and the road ahead. They made it all sound like the most natural transition in the world. After a while, she interrupted Charlie. "I need to understand how this works. How can you see Sam?" She hesitated for a moment. "And how can you see me?"

"When our accident happened," Charlie explained, "I crossed over too. It was a classic near-death experience, and when they shocked me back to life, I was graced with this gift. I could still see people in limbo between life and death."

"That's where I am now?"

"I think so," he said, "but you threw me off a little. You don't really look like most spirits."

"I'll take that as a compliment," Tess said. "Now, what about touching? How did we kiss last night? How can I open doors and change clothes and feed Bobo?"

Charlie smiled. "Right now, you have one foot in both worlds.

You're here and not here. You're literally in between." He reached out and took her hand. "Folks who die very suddenly or who don't want to let go can exert a very strong physical presence. They can do stuff like throw baseballs, drink beer, or flush toilets. They're the ones who make lights flicker and things go bump in the night."

"How come I haven't seen any?"

"Besides Sam, there aren't any around right now," he said. "Mrs. Phipps from the high school moved on this morning. And I haven't seen a firefighter named Florio in a while."

"See, God picks when you live and die," Sam added. "But when you're here in between, you have a choice too. You can stay here as long as you want, just like me. Or you can go to the next level right away. It's your call."

Tess felt a wave of worry. "Why hasn't my dad come to see me?" she asked. "I always thought he would be here waiting."

"Don't worry," Charlie said. "He'll be there for you, but you haven't crossed over to the other side yet."

"I thought this was the other side."

"That's what everyone thinks," Sam said. "They watch John Edward on TV. They read those books about the afterlife. Everyone tells you that when you die, you see the light and you pass on. Period. The end." He smiled and lowered his voice into a whisper. "It's actually more complicated."

Then he stood up and began to gesture with his hands. "There are actually lots of levels and places on this side." He drew a circle in the air. "Imagine that this is the land of the living. Marblehead is right here in the middle of everything. Your mom, your friends,

Bobo." Then he traced another circle around it. "We're right here. One level beyond. This is the middle ground."

"Think of it as the way station between life and death," Charlie said. "It's like a rest stop on the highway. I was actually there for ten minutes before the paramedic shocked me back."

"I don't get it. If this is a rest stop, what's Sam still doing here?"

The brothers looked at each other. Sam hunched his shoulders and was about to speak when Charlie cut in. "We made a promise."

"What kind of promise?"

There was a long silence. Neither of them answered. "Fine," Tess said. "Don't tell me. But am I right, Sam? You can stay here as long as you want?"

"Yes."

"Can I stay here too?"

"You're getting ahead of yourself," Charlie said.

"Yeah," Sam said. "There's time for all of that later. Right now, you've got a lot to learn."

"Go ahead," Charlie said. "Show her how it works."

"My pleasure." Sam looked up at the sky, waved his hands in a small circle, and suddenly the wind soughed through the trees. A shower of leaves swirled around them. "Not bad, huh?" he said.

"You did that?" Tess asked.

"Piece of cake. We can fill your sails. We can touch your face." He shook his hand gently, and Charlie's hair rustled.

"I never had any idea," Tess said.

"And we can dreamwalk too," Sam said.

"What's that?"

"We can go right into people's dreams. We can hang out wherever their unconscious takes them. And we can tell them stuff."

"You mean when I dream of Dad—"

"Exactly," Charlie said. "Spirits at any level can dreamwalk, even after they've crossed over."

"Are you sure?"

"You can never be sure of anything," he said, "but that's the way it seems to work."

Tess shook her head. This was too much to handle; she could scarcely breathe. She was overwhelmed. She had dreamed of her father almost every night for a year after he died. She had always thought those images were proof of how much she missed him. But now this? Was he visiting in her sleep? She didn't know what to believe anymore. And then a spark of anger ignited in her soul. She knew one thing for sure: She didn't want to spend eternity making the wind blow or wandering through people's dreams. She wanted her life back. She wanted to sail. She wanted to live. She wanted to love.

It was suddenly all quiet in the clearing. The breeze died down. And Tess gave voice to the one question that felt more important than any other: "What happens if I don't want to cross over?" She reached her hand toward Charlie. "What if I just want to stay here with you?"

"There's no rush," Charlie said. "You have all the time in the world." Then Sam got up and went to her side. He put his hand into hers and he pulled. "Come on, Tess, let's go."

"Go where?"

"I'll show you around. It's like orientation. It won't take long."

Tess wasn't sure what to do. She didn't want to go anywhere.

She just wanted to hold on to this place and this moment lest it never be the same again. Then she heard Charlie's calming voice. "Don't be afraid. When you're finished, come back to my cottage."

She looked into his caramel eyes and couldn't believe her misfortune. She knew it sounded spoony, but she had waited all her life to meet someone like him, and he had been right there all along. She had been ready to sail around the world to find her mate, and he was waiting right there in Waterside.

She felt Sam tugging. "Come on," he was saying, and she found herself walking hand in hand into the Forest of Shadows with a dead boy and his dead beagle. It boggled her mind. After a few steps, she turned back and saw Charlie silhouetted alone under the moon.

"Promise you'll be here when I get back?" she called out.

"I promise," he answered.

And then Sam looked up at her with his wide, wonderful eyes. "Don't worry, Tess," he said. "He always keeps his promises."

TWENTY-THREE

TESS WAS A NATURAL AT FLYING. ACTUALLY, "FLYING" wasn't quite the word. It didn't look anything like Superman with his arms outstretched and cape flapping. It was called spirit travel, Sam explained, and it was controlled by the mind. You only had to imagine the possibilities and you could run, swim, dive, or glide through any dimension. It was almost like using the Internet. A click here, a click there. You just had to think of a place and you were there.

For Tess, it felt like the ultimate extreme sport, with no limits on how fast or far she could go. She had never believed in any of this supernatural stuff, but soon she was soaring over downtown, circling the gilded weather vane atop Abbot Hall, then shooting down to the harbor to check out the boats.

"Sure beats PlayStation 2, huh?" Sam said as they materialized near the top of the Marblehead light.

"Blows my mind," she said, watching the powerful green beam slice right through her.

Next stop: the Sunday night submarine races on Devereux Beach, where SUVs and trucks with steamy windows were jammed into the parking lot.

"Charlie says kissing is like baseball without the bat," Sam said.

"I think it's more like football without the pads," Tess laughed. "You ever kiss a girl?"

"Nah," Sam said. "Tried once, but Stacie Bing popped me in the nose and knocked me out. I woke up in the principal's office."

"Really?"

"Swear."

"What about now? You know, in between? Is there anyone your age?"

"Not really," he said. "They don't show up here very often, and they usually move on pretty quick." He shrugged his shoulders. "Where do you want to go now?"

Tess thought for a moment. "How about my mom's?"

"Okay, lead the way."

And just like that, they found themselves near Black Joe's Pond on Gingerbread Hill. This was the hallowed ground of her youth. On this drop of water, nine generations of Carrolls had swum in the summer and skated in the winter. It was also home to a bale of snapping turtles and a siege of great blue herons.

Tess looked across the rolling lawn where as a girl she had run through the sprinklers. The family home, a charming colonial with opposing brick chimneys, sat like a toy house overlooking the pond. With a gabled roof, clapboard siding, and double-hung windows, it had barely changed since it was built by her ancestors in 1795. The downstairs lights were on in the living room, and in the window on the second floor, she saw a shaggy face. It was Bobo, looking down blankly on the grass where she was standing. He was sitting in his usual chair, still waiting for her to come home.

A car pulled into the driveway, and Tess noticed a jam of vehicles near the house.

"Wonder who's here," Tess said.

"They're your friends."

"Oh my God. What are they doing?"

"I guess they really liked you."

Once more, Tess had that overwhelmed sensation. Then she said, "Come on, let's go look."

"You sure you want to?" Sam said.

"Yeah."

"It can be a big bummer."

She recognized most of the cars, including Reverend Polkinghorne's red Subaru, and she hesitated. The last time he had been over to the house was when her dad had died. The thought of his visit the night of the heart attack brought back so many images from that first week: the steady stream of friends, the casseroles dropped off quietly on the doorstep, and the phone calls. The second week was different: Only a few friends came over, the care packages ceased, and the phone was almost silent. That was when her mom realized how alone she was in the world. Would her mother have the strength to go through it all over again?

Then she resolutely started across the grass, covering the ground in twenty steps. The side door to the mudroom was open. Her father's boots for fishing, hunting, and hiking were arranged neatly on the floor. He had been gone for two years, but her mother left them there as a comfort.

Grace was in the kitchen stirring the old chowder pot. Her face was long, her eyes were red, and her blue blouse and brown skirt didn't belong together. Her hair was primped and lacquered in a way that suggested she had sprayed it into submission just before her guests arrived. She had looked this way for weeks after Dad's funeral. When Tess had encouraged her to pay attention to herself, she had answered that she was barely clinging to her sanity and who gives a fiddler's fart about clothes?

Tess walked over and stood right beside her. She wanted to hug her so badly, but just as she reached out, Sam cut between them. "I'm sorry," he said, "but you really shouldn't."

"Why not?"

"It freaks them out."

"What do you mean? It's just a hug."

"Trust me, it scares the bejeezus out of them or it's not enough and they crave more. Either way, it just makes things worse. That's why we never touch them."

"But don't they know it's us? Can't they tell?"

"No, they don't get it. They think they're hallucinating or they end up drinking too much or popping Valium."

"But she seems so upset."

"No one's going to stop you from doing whatever you want.

You can hug her or kiss her, but eventually, you'll see there are much better ways to let her know you're here."

"Will you show me?"

"Sure, but you'll figure it out."

Tess stepped back and watched Grace finish preparing the chowder. A few of the last ingredients were laid out on the counter. It was Great-grandma Carroll's recipe, with haddock, salt pork, onions, leeks, carrots, and one pint of heavy cream. They had argued endlessly over the deadly fat in that last ingredient. For years, Grace had tried to cook more healthfully, especially for George, and she often skimped on the cream. Tess thought that was downright sacrilegious. She called it Chowder Lite, and it belonged with Diet Coke, Low-Carb Beer, and Lean Cuisine on her MOST HATED list. Whatever the consequences, she was sure that special things in life were worth all the calories and cholesterol.

Tess heard the kitchen door swing open. It was Reverend Polkinghorne, who had shown uncommon interest in Grace ever since her husband had died. As always, he was sporting the greatest hits from the L. L. Bean catalog: a blue checked sweater, tan cords, and Blucher moccasins. "You're working too hard," he said. "Won't you let me do anything? I'm very handy in the kitchen."

"You can bring some dishes into the other room." While Grace pulled bowls from the cabinet, Tess saw an opportunity. She hurried over to the stove, checked that no one was looking, and poured the pint of heavy cream into the pot. Then, out of habit, she tossed the empty carton toward the trash near the door. It banked off the rim and landed on the floor.

Grace spun around. She saw the container on the ground and walked over to it. She kneeled down, picked it up, and shook her head. "I must be losing my mind," she muttered, throwing it away. Back at the stove she gave the chowder a few stirs and touched the wooden spoon to her lips. Delicious. She went to the fridge, pulled out another carton of cream, and emptied half into the chowder. Then she churned it a few more times, picked up the pot with oven mitts, and headed into the dining room.

Tess and Sam followed. The living room was filled with friends. The ladies from the Female Humane Society were ensconced in one corner, while Bony and the guys from the wharf were sipping cider in another. Fraffie Chapman and Myrtle Sweet of the Historic District Commission were nosing around the entrance hall and examining the architectural details. *The Four Seasons* played softly on the stereo, the television flickered silently, and Bella Hooper, The Woman Who Listens, sat patiently waiting for someone who wanted to talk.

Tess moved around the room, eavesdropping on conversations, not surprised at all by what she heard. These moments were always awkward and uncomfortable, and folks carried on about the darnedest things. Fraffie and Myrtle were grousing about the historically unacceptable shag carpeting on the front stairs. Myrna Doliber, the funeral director in her helmet of black hair, was wedged on a couch with some friends relaying another superstition: "If three people are photographed together, the one in the middle will always die first."

Then in a flat, strained voice, Grace called out from the dining room: "Come 'n' get it," and she stood patiently at the buffet table ladling chowder into bowls. When everyone had been served, Reverend Polkinghorne led them all in prayer. "Let us thank God for food when others are hungry, for drink when others are thirsty, for friends when others are lonely," he began. "And may God's light surround our beloved Tess wherever she is. May God's love enfold her, God's power protect her, and God's presence watch over her. Wherever she is, God is. And may He bring her home to us safely."

"Amen."

From the corner, Tess stood and watched them devour her mom's soup. Then came the usual compliments, and she couldn't help grinning. "Wow, it's so creamy," said Todd Tucker, her favorite sail cutter from the shop. "Did you put the whole cow in here?"

"You know, the first settlers in Marblehead in 1629 made chowder with scrod," Fraffie proclaimed to no one in particular.

Grace smiled politely. She was obviously doing her best to hold it together. Her lips were pinched, and her eyes were slits. A few more visitors ooh'd and ahh'd over the chowder, and then Grace began to crack. Her fragile smile crumbled, and her eyes filled with tears. With a quick flick of her hand she wiped them away.

Tess was desperate to do something, but Sam put his hand on her shoulder. "Don't," he said. "She has to go through this. There's no other way."

Then the bell rang, and Grace hurried to the door where Tink's bulk filled the frame. He bent down to give her a big hug and followed her into the living room. The crowd quieted down to hear the latest on the search. "The last boat is back," he began.

"They found some more junk and debris. Could be thrown over from a fishing boat. Could be trash from *Querencia*."

"No sign of her yet?" Bony asked. "No radio signal? No flare?"

"Not yet, but we're going out at first light tomorrow and we'll find her."

"Why wait for tomorrow?" Grace asked. "What about now?"

"There's no point. We've got thick overcast and the moon's gone. Can't see a damn thing."

"How long do you really think she can hold on?" Grace asked.

"You know her better than anyone," Tink said. "She's a fighter. She won't give up until we find her."

Desperately, Tess looked at Sam. These poor souls were cling-ing to false hope. Then Reverend Polkinghorne jumped up from the couch, straightened his cords, and asked: "Shall we all join in another prayer?"

"No," Grace said emphatically. "No more prayers, please." She walked over to the window, wiped her eyes, and stared out into the distance.

Tess moved closer. How could it not calm her to touch her? Carefully, gently, she laid her hand on her mother's shoulder. Grace stiffened, then shuddered, whirled around, and with a look of fright in her eyes, hurried back to her guests.

"I just got the worst chill," she said to Reverend Polkinghorne. "It was just like when George died. I could swear this house is haunted."

Sadness overwhelmed Tess. "I can't stay here anymore," she said to Sam. "I've got to go. Now."

She rushed out onto the lawn under a black sky. She wanted to run as fast and as far as she could. She had never felt so powerless in her life. There was nothing she could do for her mom. There was nothing she could do for herself.

If only her father were still there. Then a terrifying thought filled her mind: What if Dad had gone through this same hell, forced to watch them suffer? Had he been there in his chair at the dining-room table for those agonizing, silent dinners? Did the dead grieve right alongside us? Did they feel our pain?

She had always been taught that they were in a better place, that they were embraced by the light, that they were with the angels. But what if that really wasn't what happened? What if the loss was just as wrenching for the dead as for the living? What if the pain never went away?

She went down to the pond and sat on a rock. Sam joined her, and they were quiet for the longest time. Then Tess asked, "Will it always feel this way?"

"No," Sam said. "It starts off pretty bad, but it changes. You'll see."

"What was your worst moment?"

Sam skipped a stone on the water. "It was right after the accident," he said. "Charlie and I were together. It was scary. Charlie had just made a promise to stay with me forever and then suddenly he began to disappear. I was stranded all alone in this weird place that turned out to be the cemetery." His voice choked up. "We figured out later on what had happened. See, we were right next to each other in between, then the paramedic shocked him back to life and he was gone." He threw another rock. Plop. "I thought I'd never see him again. I really believed it was the end."

"Then what happened?"

"It turned out all right. We still hang out every day and play catch."

"But it's not the same."

"No, it's not," he said, "but we made a promise."

"And what would happen if you—"

"Broke the promise? No way. Not gonna happen." He stomped his foot on the rock.

"Sorry," she said. "I bet you two are quite a team." She watched him for a moment and felt even more sadness. How many boys like him were out there in the ether, holding on to their big brothers and sisters who were still alive? How many husbands were floating between life and death, clinging to their wives in this world? And how many millions and millions of people were there in the world like Charlie, who couldn't let go of their loved ones when they were gone?

They sat silently by the pond and listened to the bullfrogs. In the distance, a boat engine rumbled. The night was as real as it had ever been. She heard noise on the lawn and turned to see the guests leaving. Then the lights went off in the kitchen and living room. Through the window, she watched her mother's silhouette climb the stairs. She saw her come to her bedroom window, scratch Bobo behind the ears, look out for a few moments, then close the curtains.

Tess pulled her knees close to her and wrapped herself in a ball. She felt like a fleck in the universe now. She was lost and she desperately wanted to be comforted by the only person who could help her through this lonely night.

TWENTY-FOUR

THE CHARTS WERE STREWN ALL AROUND. SO WERE THE printouts from the Weather Service and NOAA. With ruler and calculator, Charlie was reckoning where to search at dawn. He didn't care that the Coast Guard's supercomputer had crunched all the data on tides, currents, and water temperature and concluded that Tess's chances of survival were slim to none. In fact, he conceded that the situation appeared hopeless, especially since Tess's spirit had already alighted in the cemetery. But with his brain in complete denial and his heart aching, he was grasping for some other explanation of the incredible events of the last twenty-four hours.

He knew plenty of examples of miracles on the ocean, sailors subsisting for days, weeks, or even months on life rafts or lashed to wreckage. Heck, the *Hornblower* had gone down last summer on Stellwagen Bank, and fifty-five hours later they had rescued her skipper and his family from the brink, where they were bobbing in their life vests, strapped together with a green deck hose. Sure, the water was warmer, but Tess had a Gumby suit that was rated for freezing temperatures. In theory, she would have been wearing it when her boat sank, so she could still be alive.

The logs in the fireplace had burned down to embers. The time on the VCR said it was almost midnight. How did it get so late? At first he didn't notice the tree branches rustling against the window, but then they grew louder. That was strange. The cemetery had been silent all night. He stood up, straightened his T-shirt, re-tied his gray sweatpants, and adjusted one of his red wool socks. Then he went to the door, opened it, and looked outside.

Charlie's heart leaped. Tess was standing in the shadows. "God, am I glad to see you," he said, grabbing her hand and pulling her inside. She looked at him with the saddest eyes.

"I think something's happening to me," she said. "I couldn't even knock on the door. There wasn't any sound when I tried, so I had to make the wind jostle the tree branches instead."

Charlie tensed. She was losing her physical connection to this world. It was the first clue that she was fading, but he still couldn't believe it. Every single feature was as perfect as God had made it, and he couldn't detect a single sign that she was a spirit. Most ghosts had a gleam in their eyes and luminosity in their skin. Sam shimmered when the light caught him a certain way, and sometimes, when he moved quickly, the lineaments of his body blurred. But Tess was all there, every angle and curve. She stood in the middle of the darkened living room, looking at the mess of maps and weather data. He came up behind her and put his hands on her shoulders. She shuddered, turned, and looked into his eyes. She was definitely afraid. He tried to put his arms around her, but she stopped him.

"I wish we could, but Sam says it's against the rules."

"Sam? That little bugger."

"He says it's too much to handle."

"I'm willing to take that risk." His hands circled her and he pulled her close. Her body pressed hard against him, and he could tell she was soft where it mattered. She was all there in his arms. There was no mistaking it. She was real.

When they let go, she moved toward the big leather couch, plopped down in the middle, and buried herself in the pillows. "I can't frigging believe this is happening," she said. "I just can't..."

"Tell me about tonight," Charlie said, sliding in beside her.

"I went to my mom's with Sam," she said. "I couldn't take it. It was just too sad. I can't believe I put her through this again." She pulled a pillow into her lap. "My crazy friend Tink thinks he's going to rescue me tomorrow. God bless him. Poor Mom is clinging to that hope." She threw the cushion down.

Charlie put his arm around her. He could feel her shaking with every breath. And that was what seemed impossible to explain. She was a spirit and yet she was shuddering right there in his arms.

"What about you?" she said. "Where've you been tonight?"

"I went down to the dock to see what was going on." He stroked her shoulders and her hair. "Coast Guard says *Querencia* was destroyed by fire. They've been picking up charred wreckage all over Cape Ann. They think there's no way you survived."

"Do you believe that?" she asked.

"No," he said, trying to convince himself. "Not until we find your body."

Tess was staring at the burning log. "A fire..." she whispered. She seemed lost somewhere for the longest time, and then suddenly her eyes sparked and she said, "Charlie, my God. I think I remember what happened...."

The boat had been upside down forever. It was pitch black in the cabin, and the floodboards were floating around her. She was doused with diesel fuel, battery acid, and salad dressing. The water was rushing in, but she couldn't tell how much or how fast. And, most frightening of all, the boat was making the most horrible noises. *Querencia* was in agony. Tess was praying to her father to guide her through the ordeal. She was too proud to activate the EPIRB beacon or radio for help. She would tough it out until there was absolutely no other choice.

Then, like a miracle, the boat righted herself.

Thank you, Dad, wherever you are....

Tess feared that the boat had been dismasted in the rollover. She crawled through the galley, pushing pots and pans and gear out of her way. She zipped up her suit, fastened her mask, and climbed up the ladder of the companionway. At the top, she stopped for an instant to listen. She could hear the fury of the storm, but she needed to check the rigging. She held her breath and opened the hatch.

The pressure changed instantly as the wind burst inside along with a gush of seawater. She quickly hooked her tether onto the jack line and pulled herself on deck. The sky and sea had merged into one great wall of white, and it felt like she was flying.

She wasn't sure she could stand upright in the high winds, so she stayed in a crouch as she scanned *Querencia* for damage.

Sure enough, the mast had been sheared like a toppled tree from the deck, leaving only a jagged stump of carbon-fiber splinters. The remains of the pole, fastened by halyards, were swinging from the boat and slamming into it like a battering ram with every ransacking wave. Tess knew she had to chop them loose immediately or they would pierce the hull, and she would founder.

The boat was pitching violently. She scooted to the cabin locker and pulled the bolt-cutters from the bracket. It took all her strength to slice through the stainless-steel rod rigging and to sever the main halyard, two jibs, and spinnaker. Instantly, a massive wave swept the mast away.

Then she duckwalked to the cockpit and surveyed her instruments.

Damn!

The autopilot was off. How long ago did that happen? Must have been when she lost power. She punched the button to get it going again, but it was out. She tried the backup. It was gone too. Now there was no choice: She would have to steer her way through this. But where the heck was she? She peered at the compass, trying to get her bearings. North. South. East...

Before she could finish, a wave smashed into the rear deck, slamming her hard against the wheel. It knocked the wind out of her, and she bent over, gasping for breath. A thunderous boom overhead made her stand right up. She looked to the heavens and saw a brilliant flash, then a zigzagging web of lightning. It spread out like lace across the sky. Even in the maelstrom, she appreciated its beauty. But she also knew the lightning rod had been swept away with the mast and with it her only protection.

She leaned back toward the controls and tried to calculate her location. She had been running without steering for a few hours. It was hard to tell which way the wind and current had carried her, but she estimated that she was somewhere between—

Tess never finished the thought. The boat breached violently, and she toppled toward the lifelines. She skidded along the deck, slammed into a stainless-steel stanchion, then felt her safety harness cutting hard into her ribs. Now she was lying flat on the deck, staring up into the darkness.

Her side ached, and she wondered how long the boat could take this beating. She pulled herself back to her feet, inched toward the cabin, and peered inside. The water had already swallowed the bunks and was rising fast.

It was a surreal moment, but Tess recognized it was time literally to abandon ship. Every good offshore sailor knew that you waited until the last possible moment and never got into a life raft unless you were stepping *up* into it from a sinking ship. Indeed, many sailors had perished over the years by deserting boats that

managed to stay afloat, only to be swamped by the seas in an in-
flatable dinghy. But *Querencia* was going down. So she pulled the
cord on the thick bundle strapped in the back of the cockpit, the
CO_2 canister hissed, and the raft began to inflate.

Now she had two choices: hurry below and activate the
distress signal, or stay above and contact the Coast Guard on
Channel 16, the emergency frequency. The radio in the cockpit
was faster and, incredibly, it was unscathed. She reached for the
mike.

Before she could even say "Mayday," without any warning of
thunder, a lightning bolt slammed into the deck. Tess felt the
blast of heat from an explosion, then saw fire on the starboard
side of the boat where the fuel tank was stored. Even in this tem-
pest, the flames leaped high in the air.

Suddenly, the boat pitched to starboard, Tess lost her footing,
and she felt the full force of her body slam against the jack line.
For an instant, she was dangling upside down over the transom.
Then she felt the safety wire snap and the tension release on her
harness. Now there was nothing keeping her on the boat. She began to slide into the churning ocean.

In that instant, dragged away by the waves, she looked back at
her beloved boat, and those were the last images she could remember: *Querencia* on fire and the white sky and sea closing in all
around.

TWENTY-FIVE

"WOULD YOU EVER LEAVE SAM?"

Tess's question lingered in the glow of the fireplace. Perhaps they were simply in denial about the facts or maybe they were swept away by each other, but they had abandoned the gloomy subject of the shipwreck and were dreaming out loud about what life would be like together.

"Would you ever leave the cemetery?" Tess asked. Her face was tucked into Charlie's neck. "I mean, would you ever come with me around the world?" She couldn't believe she was asking the question, but it was true. She didn't want to go solo anymore. She wanted to be with him.

"You've never seen me sail," he said. "Be careful what you wish for."

"Don't joke. I'm being serious." Then she found

herself asking a question that seemed almost too direct: "Are you going to stay here forever with Sam?"

Charlie stroked her hair. "Remember that bullfighting book I told you about?" She nodded. "There's a pass called *al alimón*, where two matadors challenge a bull while holding on to the sides of just one cape. It's suicide unless they're in perfect harmony. In Spain, they say that only two brothers know each other's thoughts and movements well enough to pull it off."

"You and Sam."

"I couldn't face life without him."

He kissed her softly on the forehead, and she felt safe enough to ask once more, "So what about us? What's going to happen to you and me?"

He pulled her closer. "trust your heart / if the seas catch fire," he whispered, reciting the poem from her father's funeral.

"(and live by love / though the stars walk backward)," she answered.

"That's what I want to do with the time we have." He kissed her gently on the cheek. Then he whispered, "Come with me." He slipped from the couch and stood up.

Tess watched him beckon and she didn't know what to do. One candle was still burning on the coffee table. The fire was out. The room was silent.

"Come upstairs," he said. "I won't bite."

"We can't," Tess said as the sadness returned. "It's impossible. I couldn't even knock on the door. I'm not really here."

"Can you feel this?" he said, leaning forward and kissing her on the corner of her eye.

"Of course."

"Can you feel this?" he said, running his hand across her shoulders and down to her breasts.

"Yes."

"You're still in between. You haven't crossed over yet. Anything is possible."

"Pretty smooth," she said. "So this is how you get into a ghost's pants?" She poked him in the ribs. Then he took the candle from the table and crossed the living room. "This way," he said.

Tess followed through the darkness, up a steep staircase, down a little hall into his room. It was small and cozy, with a vaulted ceiling and exposed beams. A big craftsman bed took up almost all the space. He set the candle on the nightstand.

In the low light she could see Charlie take off his T-shirt and dive onto the bed. Below his muscled chest and stomach, his sweatpants were enticingly low on his waist. A small part of her wanted to play hard to get and make him work. It was a reflex from years of experience and disappointment. But that was ridiculous. This wasn't the time for games. It was now or never.

"Tell me the truth," she said. "Have you ever done something like this before?"

"You mean sleep with a spirit on a second date?" He was flashing that incredible dimple.

"Don't push your luck, pal." She pulled the clip from her hair, and it fell around her shoulders. She began to unbutton her shirt. And suddenly she noticed. The lines of her hands were softer. Her skin was fainter. Even the feeling of her clothes was different. Everything was less substantial. It took a moment to process, but then she realized.

She was beginning to fade away.

It filled her with pure terror. This was really, truly the end. Soon she would evanesce to nothing. It made no sense. Sam had promised the timing would be her decision. She had made up her mind: She didn't want to go yet. She wanted to stay right here with Charlie.

"Hey, what's taking so long?" he said.

"Calm down, boy." She didn't know what to do, but there he was with his arms open. And so she finished the last buttons of her shirt and kicked off her shoes. She dashed over to the bed and blew out the candle. She didn't want him to see her this way. She didn't want him to know it was already happening.

Then she dived onto him, feeling his warmth against her own. Their fingers touched, and they were together, his arms encircling her waist, and her hands moving around his neck. Their kiss was deep, connecting, like a familiar story with a beginning, middle, and end. They caught their breath, and then she kissed his forehead, face, and shoulders.

Now her hands were on his chest, her fingers gliding along the faint ridges of what seemed like scars. "What're these from?" she asked.

"Burn marks when the paramedic shocked me."

She kissed each one gently and then moved lower, gliding her mouth over his stomach and hips, untying his sweatpants, sliding them off. Then her hands wrapped around him, all heat and power, and she reveled in a new discovery: He was the most perfect man she had ever touched.

She didn't want to let go, but he rolled her over onto her back, unzipped her jeans, and in one fluid motion lifted her up to pull them off. His strength was impressive, and his instincts were very, very good.

He handled her as if she was weightless, and her anxiety began to melt away. After kissing for the longest time, they began to fold into each other slowly and smoothly, and she felt him fill her completely. For the first time ever, venturing deeper, Tess lost her sense of where she ended and he began.

When it was over, they held on to each other with all their strength. Tess was afraid even to loosen her grip. She was clinging to love and life. Soon Charlie was ready again, and they found their rhythm. This time she dissolved into a sublime state that she had not even known in her younger, wilder days. With sparks between every synapse and energy in every cell, the sensation was surreal, like the bliss she had always dreamed of and had almost given up hope of ever finding.

Afterward, with Charlie resting his head on her stomach, she felt the tears begin to well up, then spill.

"Please don't cry," he said.

"I can't help it. I want to stay here with you. I don't want to go."

"Don't worry," he said. "There's no rush."

But in the shadowed bedroom, he had not seen her fading form. She ran her hands through his hair and rubbed his sinuous back. She pulled him toward her once more. She didn't want to waste a single moment. There was no time to rest or sleep, for in her heart and soul she knew they would only have tonight.

★   ★   ★

There's no rush...

The lies we tell ourselves, Charlie thought as he kissed her nape and followed the muscles of her neck down to her shoulders and breasts. He cupped one and then the other. They were so warm in his hands, and then his mouth.

She was right there—arching, twisting beneath him—and yet he knew this rapture was fleeting, and it only made him more ravenous. He ran his tongue along her ribs, over her stomach, down her sides, marveling at her nooks and curves. He kissed the points of her hips, then her thighs, and she curled up in giggles.

"No fair," she murmured.

"All's fair," he answered.

Earlier, when she had flopped on the bed and they had joined together, it had felt like some mysterious experiment. Could they really touch, let alone make love? Was this even possible? With disbelief and tentativeness, they had pushed against each other, like force fields, a flurry of friction and energy, mouth against mouth, hand vs. hand.

Now, this time, as he eased into her again, they merged ineffably. The resistance was gone, and so was the distance. Their bodies coalesced in ways he could not fathom, and the sensation was stirring and soulful.

And so, sweeping aside the impossibility of their union, Charlie pushed deeper and deeper into her until he was completely gone.

TWENTY-SIX

THE TRADE WINDS ROCKED THEM GENTLY IN THE HAM-
mock. The flag on the mast of the Catalina 400 rippled. They were anchored somewhere in the cays off
the coast of Belize. Sipping from a coconut, Tess was
nuzzled up against Charlie. She offered him the straw,
he took a sweet sip, and he kissed her lips and throat.
He could smell the tanning lotion, sea salt, and that
unmistakable scent that was just hers.

Now she was above him, moving in a swirl of motion, caressing him all over. Now they were swinging
more, the hammock wobbling, and the coconut drink
flying, bouncing across the deck into the ocean. Now
she was all around him, pulling, pressing, dancing to
some inner music.

It was fast at first, then it turned slower. The swaying in the hammock ceased. Their faces were side by side. Her mouth was open. Tendrils of hair draped over his chest. Her breathing was strong, and she made little sounds that were not quite whimpers. Then her intensity began to grow, and her arms tightened around him. Her hips were pushing harder. She put one hand behind his neck.

"I love you," she said, her eyes reflecting the sun and sky.

Just as he was about to swear his love, Charlie heard clanging. He lifted his head and looked down the length of the boat. An American flag fluttered at the stern. They were all alone, but there was more clanging, like someone beating a pan. "What's that?" he asked, but Tess didn't answer. Her eyes were distant now. She suddenly seemed far away. He struggled to make sense of the noise. Then a man's voice called out.

"St. Cloud! Charlie! Hello?!"

The words shook him from his dream. He opened his eyes and rolled over. He reached out for Tess.

But she was gone.

"Tess?!" His heart ached as he leaped from bed to the window. Outside, silver sheets of rain obscured the cemetery. That racket had to be Tink down on the dock, clanging the bell on the post. A century ago, the clamor was the fastest way to summon the gravediggers when a casket from the North Shore had arrived by boat.

"Okay, okay!" he grumbled. "Give it a rest! I'll be right there!" He turned and grabbed his clothes from the chair. And there it was.

A note on the pillow.

His pulse quickened as he unfolded the piece of paper.

My dearest Charlie,

As I write this note, I can barely see my hands or hold this pen. By the time you open your eyes in the morning, I know you won't be able to see me anymore. That is why I must go before you wake.

I'm sorry to leave without saying good-bye, but it's easier this way. I don't want you to see this happening to me. . . . I just want you to remember our time together.

I had hoped to stay longer. There's so much we could have done. I only wish we had cooked a few more meals, gone to a ball game—Patriots, of course—or even sailed the world. But I'll never forget how you opened my heart and made me feel more alive than I ever dreamed possible.

Sam told me that the timing of moving on was my decision. But apparently it's not. I wanted to stay close to you but I can't anymore.

I hate the thought of leaving, but I'm hopeful about what's to come. I'm not afraid. You see, I think we were destined to meet. There's a reason for everything, you said, and though it's a mystery to me now, I know it won't always be so.

Someday, we'll be together. I believe that with all my heart. Until then, I want you to dive for dreams. I want you to trust your heart. I want you to live by love. And when you're ready, come find me. I'll be waiting for you.

With all my love,
Tess

Charlie felt the numbness spread from his fingers up his arms and all the way through his body. Dammit. When had he fallen asleep? How could he have let her go?

He threw on his clothes, folded the note, and put it in his shirt pocket. Tink was still clanging the bell on the dock. Charlie ran down the stairs and straight out the door. He didn't even bother to grab a coat. He raced across the lawn, weaving between monuments, splashing through the puddles. When he got to the dock, Tink was in a lather.

"Been waiting here for twenty frigging minutes!" he said. "What took you so long?"

"I'm sorry," Charlie said. The rain was cold, and he was shivering in his T-shirt.

"You ready? Forget your coat?"

"It's too late," Charlie said.

"Too late? For what? You're the only one who's late."

"There's no point anymore." The water was streaming down his face and arms.

"What're you talking about?"

"Tess is gone."

"Did Hoddy call you or something? Last night you were the one who said we can't give up on her."

"I know," he said, brushing the rain from his face. "I was wrong."

"What the heck are you talking about?"

"You won't find her out there. She's gone."

"Dammit, St. Cloud, you're out of your mind." He gunned the boat engine. "I'm going without you. And screw you for wasting my time." He pushed away from the dock and cursed as he steered into the channel.

Charlie stood for the longest time, soaked by the freezing rain. He watched Tink's boat disappear into the mist. Slowly, he felt himself steeling inside. The emotional fortifications were going up. The defenses and buttresses were moving into place. And just as he had done for thirteen years, he forced his mind to ignore the hurt.

It was Monday morning. The week was starting. His workers would be arriving soon. There were graves to dig. Hedges to cut. Headstones to set. And when the day was done, his little brother would be waiting.

Nothing had changed. Everything had changed.

TWENTY-SEVEN

IT WAS A MISERABLE DAY, EVEN FOR A FUNERAL. ABRAHAM Bailey, one of the richest men in town, had died in his sleep, and Charlie, bundled against the wind, was on Eastern Slope, dressing the grave. Good old Abe had made it to 101 years old. In the morbid calculus of the cemetery workers, that meant the coffin would be lighter and the job therefore easier. Centenarians never weighed much.

Charlie shrugged his shoulders at the thought. Those were the kind of grim facts he would have to ponder every day for the rest of his life. Along with the iron gates and stone walls, they were the bleak realities that immured the cemetery, like the chill in the air. He dreaded the frigid months ahead, not least because the cemetery was actually colder than anyplace in the entire county. In summer, all that marble and granite stored the heat and raised the temperature, but when winter came with snow and rain, the stone held the frost and made it worse.

Charlie now slogged through every step by rote. He dug the hole with precisely twenty-six scoops of the backhoe. He covered the dirt pile with Astroturf. He installed the lowering device.

With every action, memory fragments exploded in his mind: Tess's eyes, her laugh, her legs. Down the hill was the lake where he had first seen her. Stop! Pay attention to the job, he admonished himself. Set up the tent. Put out the chairs. Arrange the floral tributes.

Deep down, he felt some strange kind of motion sickness, like he had lost his balance or his rhythm. His world of obelisks and mausoleums seemed unstable, and he steadied himself on his shovel. He peered into the muddy ground that he had opened. It wasn't his most careful work. The earthen walls weren't even, but only he knew how they should look. He brushed away a few stray clumps of dirt and smoothed the surface around the opening.

Next, he pulled the lopping shears from his cart. It was time to tame some of the wild shrubs that so infuriated Fraffie Chapman and the Historic District Commission. Old Charlie would have ignored their demands for another year or two, but New Charlie didn't care anymore. There was no point. He would start the clipping job before the Bailey funeral and then would bring the rest of the workers over to finish it off. He reached into the low branches of the bushes, cut out some dead leaves, trimmed a few inches from the top, and shaved some more from the side.

Then he stopped.

His will was broken. His edge was gone. He had lost his drive. The tape-recorded bells in the Chapel of Peace began to ring. He listened. And remembered. Walking under the moon. Making love in the candlelight. The images rolled on, merging with the murk in his head and blurring gray like the cloud cover. For thirteen years, he had been inured to the pain and drudgery of this place, but how could he possibly dig and mow for forty more? Did he really want to spend his whole life here, only to be buried near his brother with a bronze Weedwacker for his memorial? How was he supposed to pretend that life was any good without Tess?

His eye caught sight of a big man lumbering up the hill, moving between the tombstones. The afternoon light filtered right through him. His hair was neatly combed and gelled, but the contours of his fireman blues were gauzy. It was Florio Ferrente, the firefighter, and he was fading.

"Greetings," he said.

"Hey, haven't seen you in a few days."

"Been real busy," Florio said, "trying to look after the wife and son."

Charlie leaned his shears against a monument. "How're they holding up?"

"Not so good. It's been real rough. Francesca isn't sleeping. The baby won't stop crying."

"I'm so sorry."

"So I got a question for you, Charlie." Florio seemed ten years younger and twenty pounds lighter. He was ready to move on. "I need to know, Charlie. How long does this last? You know, the pain? When Francesca hurts, I hurt too. It's like we're connected."

"You are connected," Charlie said, "and it lasts until you and your family release each other." He paused. "Some folks get there sooner than others."

"What about you?" Florio asked. His eyes were serious. "You think you got everything figured out?"

"I guess so. Why?"

"Just wondering." Florio looked Charlie up and down, then put his hat on his head and adjusted the brim. The light flowed through him.

"What's your point?" Charlie asked.

"I've just been thinking a lot," he said. "All my life, I went to church and read Ecclesiastes. You know, where it says there's a time for everything and a season for every activity under heaven. A time to weep and laugh, to love and hate, to search and give up." He paused. "Trust me, Charlie. The Bible got it wrong. There isn't time in a man's life for everything. There isn't a season for every activity."

There were tears in his eyes, and he wiped them away with a shimmering slab of a hand. "Remember the end of my funeral? Father Shattuck said, 'May he rest in peace.' What a crock! I don't want to rest. I want to live." He shook his head. "But there isn't time for that. Know what I mean?"

"I do."

Florio looked across the vast lawn studded with granite. "I guess I better get going."

"You sure you don't want to stay?"

"No," Florio said. "Just watch out for my family, okay? Keep an eye on Francesca and the boy."

"I promise."

They shook hands, and Florio pulled him into an embrace. He hadn't been hugged by a guy this size in years. When they let go, Charlie saw the sparkle of a gold amulet around Florio's neck and recognized the engraved figure of Jude, patron saint of desperate situations, carrying an anchor and an oar.

Florio grabbed Charlie's arm. "Remember, God chose you for a reason." Then he walked away, a gleaming mountain of a man, disappearing among the monuments.

"You sure about this?" Joe the Atheist said, punching his time card in the box. "It's only three P.M." The rest of the guys were lined up behind him in the service yard to clock out. Charlie had called everyone in from the field to give them the rest of the day off.

"You got a problem going home early?" Charlie said. "I'm sure I can find something for you to do."

"No," Joe said. "I'm good. I'll just be the first one at the Rip Tide today. You want to come along?"

"No, thanks," Charlie said.

"You doing okay, Chucky boy?" Joe said. "You really don't look so hot."

"I'm fine. See you tomorrow."

Charlie knew he wasn't doing a very good job of hiding his distress. It wasn't like him to call it quits so early on a Monday, the busiest day of the week. As a rule, most folks tended to die from heart attacks today. The coronaries usually came from hard living over the weekend or the stress of the work-week ahead. By afternoon, the burial requests from the funeral homes always started to arrive. It was true in cemeteries around the world.

But he was done with work for the day. He didn't care if the orders went unfilled or the boxwoods and yews ran wild.

And so after his last employee clocked out, Charlie drove the little cart to the cottage by the forest. He went straight to his armchair, plunked himself down with a half bottle of Jack Daniel's. He stared at the wall right in front of him with the maps and circles that defined his life.

Twilight tonight would come at 6:29 P.M.

He guzzled one shot and poured himself another. This wasn't like him either. He rarely drank and certainly not alone. But he wanted the pain to go away. He drained the second glass and poured a third. Soon his head was swimming and swirling through wild thoughts.

He was done with cutting lawns. He was done digging graves. The bliss of loving Tess, the exhilaration of the last few days, had made him realize how much he had sacrificed and squandered over the years. It was almost as if Sam hadn't been the only one to die in the accident. Charlie had forfeited his own life too.

He thought about Sam and the promise. At first, the gift had seemed the greatest blessing. But now he understood. He and his kid brother were both trapped in the twilight. They were mirror images, clinging to each other, holding each other back from what awaited them beyond the great iron gates.

This was the end. He was finished with waiting for sundown every night to play catch with a loving ghost. He was through with the boundaries of those circles on the map. And most of all, he was done with being alone.

Florio was right. He had been given a second chance. And he had wasted it.

At first, the solution came to him as a faint glimmer. Something like it had crossed his mind thirteen years earlier when Sam had died. Back then he had pushed the answer into the dark caverns of his mind where it had belonged. But now the idea made another dramatic entrance. This time it seemed almost irresistible.

Come find me, Tess had written in her note. The answer was right there in her letter. If he couldn't be with her on earth, then why not join her out there somewhere? Why not give up this world for the next? It would be over quickly. It would put an end to all the pain. Most important, he and Tess would spend forever together. And he could keep his promise by bringing Sam along to the next level.

He swallowed another gulp of whiskey and felt the burning in his throat. Was this so crazy? Would anyone really miss him on earth? No. His mother was all the way across the country with her new life and family. She probably wouldn't even notice if he was gone.

So what was he waiting for?

He got up and walked to the maps. He ripped them from the walls. He wouldn't need them where he was going. The room was spinning fast now. He reached out for a lamp to steady himself, but he lost his balance and fell to the ground. He landed with a thud, and his head slammed into the wood floor. He lay there stunned for a few moments and tried to focus his bewildered mind. He couldn't even remember what he had just been thinking about. His vision was fuzzy, and his head throbbed.

Then the thought came back to him again. It was the perfect solution to his problems, and only one question remained to be answered:

How would he take his own life?

TWENTY-EIGHT

COME FIND ME . . .

When Charlie awoke, he saw the words right there in front of him on Tess's note. His body ached, and he had an awful taste of booze in his mouth. Coruscating shafts of light angled down from the windows. The dismal rain had obviously cleared. He looked around and saw the mess on the floor: destroyed maps, shredded sunset tables, the empty bottle of Jack Daniel's.

He sat up and rubbed his head. What time was it? He checked the clock over the fireplace. 5:35 P.M. Wow, he had been out for almost an hour. The last thing he remembered was ripping everything from the wall. Then he must have passed out.

Through the grogginess, a sliver of a dream, tantalizingly incomplete, lingered in his consciousness. He was on the water in a storm. The waves were high and rolling. He was in a Coast Guard cutter. And that was all. The rest was just out of reach. He tried to bring it into focus, but the memory eluded him. The whiskey was blurring everything.

He scooped up the torn scraps on the floor. Like a simple puzzle, he put together three ripped pieces of the chart covering the North Shore from Deer Island and Nahant around the Cape to Plum Island and Newburyport. Then he reassembled four scraps of paper stretching from Hampton Beach to Cape Elizabeth, including Boon Island and Cape Porpoise.

Looking around again he saw that surprisingly one chart had survived his attack and lay apart with a ray of sunlight glancing across the Isles of Shoals. A draft of air nudged the page toward him, and Charlie wondered: Was Tess trying to signal him or lead the way? He grabbed the map and turned it around and around. It showed the area from Provincetown to Mt. Desert Island, Maine, and the stretch from Cape Ann all the way across Bigelow Bight. He studied the contours of the coast and ran his finger over the little islands five miles offshore.

The adrenaline surged, and the hangover instantly was gone. His mind was racing. Did Tess leave the map for him to see? Was this a message? Or was this flat-out drunken craziness?

He hugged the chart to his chest. As a boy, he had sailed every inch of that rugged coastline. He had explored the nine rocky outcroppings of the Isles of Shoals and had climbed to the very top of the old White Island Light. He knew where the waters were shallow and the ledges were hidden at high tide, and on countless fishing trips there he had caught bushels of mackerel and bluefish.

Come find me . . .

These desolate islands off the border of New Hampshire and Maine were nowhere near the Coast Guard's search area. In fact, the first wreckage had been picked up eighteen nautical miles due south off Halibut Point, and the burned life raft had been floating even farther away.

It was incredible: They had been searching in the wrong spot.

How could he have missed it? What a fool! Tess was waiting for him. And he had already wasted a day.

Charlie jumped up and seized the phone. He would call Hoddy Snow first and then alert the Coast Guard. Dear God, please make them listen. Maybe it wasn't too late. He dialed the numbers and heard La-Dee-Da pick up.

"Harbormaster's office, may I help you?"

"It's Charlie St. Cloud. I need to speak with Hoddy. It's urgent."

"Hold, please."

"I can't hold—"

He heard the Muzak. Damn. There wasn't any time. They needed to get out there right away. Then he tried to plan out exactly what he would say: He had reason to believe that Tess was still out there on the water. Her spirit had left him a note. She was calling out to him.

He heard Hoddy's gruff voice. "Hello? What's the big deal, St. Cloud?"

Charlie hung up. It was preposterous, really. Hoddy would think he was out of his mind, and maybe he was. An hour ago, he was thinking about taking his own life.

He felt a surge of desperation. He went to the window. The

sun was starting to drop in the western sky. He couldn't miss the sunset with Sam. But what about Tess?

He was hyperventilating now, and his head was feeling dizzy. *Take a deep breath,* he told himself. *Think, Charlie, think.* There had to be a way he could have both.

Then he remembered Florio's gravelly voice: "God had a reason for saving you. He had a purpose." And "Don't worry, son. Sometimes it takes a while to figure things out. But you'll hear the call. You'll know when it's time. And then, you'll be set free."

Perhaps this was his moment. Maybe this was the call. In that instant, everything became clear. Charlie knew exactly what he had to do. So he grabbed his coat, flew out the door, and took off across the cemetery.

IV

TRUE WIND

TWENTY-NINE

THE BOW OF THE *HORNY TOAD* SCUDDED ALONG THE
waves. Charlie stood on the tower of the twenty-eight-
foot Albemarle sportfishing boat and steered into the
gloaming. The twin diesel engines were cranked up at
full thrust, and in the cockpit, Tink bounced along
with his stomach jiggling and his shaggy hair blowing
wild in the wind. Below on the back deck, Joe the
Atheist shivered and sobered up faster than he would
have liked.

When Charlie had finally found Joe at the Rip Tide,
he was wobbling on a stool, well into his fourth shot of
Jim Beam, telling a story to no one in particular. It was
half past five and the place was clogged with cliques of
happy-hour regulars—town workers just off the clock
and fishermen fresh from the water.

"Charlie!" someone had called out. "Come over here, St. Cloud," said another.

He had felt an arm on his shoulder pulling him toward a booth where the guys from the Board of Health were sharing a pitcher. With a hard elbow, he managed to shake loose and push his way to the bar. He grabbed Joe's stool and spun him around.

"I need a favor," Charlie had said.

"Bartender!" Joe shouted. "Another round for my friend—" His eyes were webbed with broken capillaries, and his speech was slurred.

"I need the *Horny Toad*," Charlie said.

Joe had lurched back and yelled out to the cemetery workers in the back. "Hey, fellas! The boss wants my—"

Charlie had grabbed him by the collar. "I don't have time for this. Tell me where your boat is. I'll have it back tomorrow morning."

"You're going out all night without inviting me?"

"Just give me the keys. If anything happens, I promise I'll pay you back."

"Where you going? I want to know."

"Please, Joe."

"Answer's no," he had said, crossing his tattooed arms.

Charlie's heart had sunk. He didn't have time or options. Who else was going to lend him a speedboat? And then, he lost control, grabbing Joe by the collar, pulling him in so close he could smell the bourbon and tobacco. The room stood still.

"Goddammit, I'm taking your boat!"

"Goddammit?" Joe hissed. "Who do you think you're talking

to? I don't buy that baloney, remember?" Nobody in the bar had moved. Their faces were just inches apart. Then Joe had burst out laughing. "C'mon, St. Cloud, let's get out of here. Wherever you're going, I'm coming with you."

Joe had slammed his glass on the counter, lunged off the stool, and stumbled toward the door. On the way to the boat, Charlie had grabbed his foul-weather gear from the back of his Rambler, while Joe rummaged around in his Subaru and unearthed a party-size bag of Doritos and a pint of Old Crow.

On the dock, Tink was dejectedly coiling his lines after a day of futile searching. His only sightings—some melted shards of fiberglass and charred seat cushions—were bad omens that the fire on *Querencia* had burned all the way through the hull.

"You were right," Tink had said. "It's too late."

"No, I was wrong," Charlie had answered. "It's not too late. She's still out there. She's waiting for us."

"Are you frigging kidding me?" His face was filled with anger. "Don't screw with me, St. Cloud. I'm not in the mood."

"I'm serious, Tink. I think I know where she is. Come with us. What've you got to lose?"

"My sanity, but it's probably too late for that...." Tink lifted his duffel and cooler, and hopped onto the *Horny Toad*.

Now Charlie aimed the prow on a 55-degree heading toward the Gloucester sea buoy. They were doing 25 knots, and if the wind stayed behind them, they would be able to pick it up to 30 once they got around the tip of Cape Ann. At this speed, Charlie calculated it would take an hour.

And then what? Charlie knew the moon was waning, and

heavy clouds would block out any light. But it didn't matter. He was counting on his high beam and flares. He would find Tess.

To starboard, a noisy booze cruise heading out on the sunset run pulsated with the music and laughter of a party on the top deck. As the *Horny Toad* zoomed past, two revelers leaning against the railing lifted their beer bottles in a silent toast.

Soon they were clear of coastal traffic, and Charlie pushed the throttle all the way forward.

"What's the big hurry?" Joe said, hauling himself woozily up the ladder. "It's not like you're really going to find that Carroll girl." He hiccuped. "In fact, I'll bet you fifty big ones that we'll dig that girl's grave this week."

Charlie felt his temper flare. "Shut your drunk mouth," he said. He never should have taken Joe along for the ride, but it was the price of using the boat, one of the fastest in the harbor.

"Well, I'll be damned," Joe said after a while. "You had some secret thing going with that girl, didn't you?"

"Drop it, Joe. Please?"

He glanced at Tink, checked the compass, and aimed the boat on a 44-degree heading for the Cape Ann sea buoy. Joe burped, waved his hand dismissively, and grumbled to himself. Charlie looked back over his shoulder and saw the PG&E smokestacks in Salem receding in the hazy distance. A flock of herring gulls was following in their wake. Then he checked his watch.

Incredible. It was already 6:20 P.M. He turned to Tink. "Take the wheel for a minute?"

"You bet." He stepped forward and put both hands on the wood. Then Charlie climbed down the ladder and went to the stern. He stood there for a long time staring toward the west. Water and land merged in the twilight, a wedge of gray against the sky. The sun had slumped below the horizon.

Charlie felt the tears well up.

It was the first time in thirteen years that he would miss the game of catch with Sam. He thought about dusk in the hidden playground, where the plate and mound would be as empty as he felt. He imagined his little brother showing up and waiting all by himself on the wood swing. God, he hoped Sam would understand. . . .

The view before him was changing colors, like slides on a screen. There were great strokes of purple on the horizon mixed with slashes of blue and white. He tried to savor the magnificence of the moment. For all those years, he had only seen the sun disappear between the trees in the forest. He remembered the aspen and poplars silhouetted against the light, like slats on a window or bars in a jail. That was his frame of reference, his one perspective on the passage of day into night.

Now the whole world was before him, and he gasped at the vast beauty of it all. He breathed the damp and salty air. He heard the seagulls cry. Storm petrels and common terns drifted low on the water. And the sky dissolved once more into bands of blue and gray until everything was black.

It was night.

"Good-bye, Sam," he whispered.

The wind was cold, and the dark swallowed up his farewell. Then he turned and climbed the ladder back to the bridge. There were stars in the sky ahead, and he knew one thing for sure. Tess was out there waiting for him, and he would not let her down.

THIRTY

THEY WERE SMACK IN THE MIDDLE OF THE ISLES OF SHOALS, between Smuttynose and Star Islands. Charlie reached for the searchlight and hit the switch. The beam sliced the darkness, and its white point glanced off the water. He swung it around in a big circle. A flying fish skittered across the surface.

A night of desperate searching stretched ahead.

He and Tink took turns at the wheel, trolling the ocean, sweeping the emptiness with the light, calling out until their voices were hoarse. Joe woke up around 3:00 A.M. and pitched in for an hour, steering while Charlie and Tink stood watch. With each brush of the searchlight, with every advancing second, his heart sank even further. Was he wrong about the clues? Was this all a creation of his grief? "Give me a sign, Tess," he prayed. "Show me the way."

There was only silence.

As dawn came at 6:43 A.M., the east began to glow with stripes of orange and yellow. But the arrival of this new day meant only the worst for Charlie. He had risked everything and he had lost. Sam would be gone. All that was left was a job in the cemetery mowing the lawn and burying the dead. He had turned something into nothing, and he had only himself to blame.

His back ached from standing watch. His stomach growled from lack of food. His head hurt from a night of crying out into the gloom. What should he do next? He searched for a sign from Sam and wondered if his little brother was okay.

Then he heard Joe down below, grumbling and grunting as he climbed the ladder. "I'm sorry," he said. "I must've nodded off." His voice was raspy from sleep. "Any luck?"

"None."

"Well, you did your best," he said, reaching for the wheel and elbowing Charlie aside. "I'm the captain of this boat and I say we go home."

"It's just getting light," Charlie protested. "Maybe we missed her last night." He turned to Tink. "What do you say? Where should we look now?"

Joe interrupted: "Face it, Charlie. I know you had to get this out of your system, but she's gone."

"No! She's alive." He felt crazed inside. His frantic brain searched for examples. "There was that sailor who was unconscious for nine days in the Bering Sea. Remember him? He was on the news. A Japanese whaler picked him up and he survived."

"Right." Joe had turned the boat around.

"Cold water slows your metabolism." Charlie barely recognized his own voice. "It's the mammalian dive reflex. Your body knows how to shut down everything except for essential functions and organs." It was the only thing left to hold on to. "Remember those climbers on Everest a few years ago? They were above twenty-seven thousand feet in the death zone. They were lost, frostbitten, and slipped into comas. But they managed to survive."

"You crazy or something?" Joe said. "Those climbers were lucky, that's all."

"It wasn't luck. It was a miracle."

"How many times do I have to tell you? There's no such thing."

Joe pushed forward on the throttle, and the boat leaped for home. Charlie knew it was over. Numbly, he made his way down the ladder to the stern, where he plunked down on one of the benches and drowned his thoughts in the drone of the engine.

As he stared at the wake spreading out behind him, the sun climbed the sky, bathing the ocean in a soft glow. But Charlie felt an aching cold inside. His fingers trembled, his body shivered, and he wondered if he would ever be warm again.

THIRTY-ONE

SAM WAS WIND.

He whooshed across the Atlantic, skimming the wave tops, reveling in the most amazing feeling. He was liberated from the in between, and the parameters of his new playground were dazzlingly infinite—the universe with its forty billion galaxies and all the other dimensions beyond consciousness or imagination. His quietus had finally brought freedom. No longer constricted by his promise, he had moved on to the next level, where he could morph into any shape.

Sam was now a free spirit.

But there was one more thing he had to do on earth. He swept over the bow of the *Horny Toad* and swirled around his brother, trying to get his attention, but to no avail. Another loop around the boat and another breezy pass, with a good gust whipping the American flag on its pole, flipping Charlie's hair, and filling his jacket, but again he had no luck. Then he twanged the guy wires of the boat, making an eerie, wailing song, but Charlie didn't hear a single note.

Last night, Sam had felt annoyed and betrayed by Charlie's abrupt departure from the cemetery. At sundown, he had hung around the Forest of Shadows, waiting and waiting. Loneliness had overwhelmed him as the purple light vanished from the sky, and the hidden playground had grown dark. Soon anger began to creep in as he realized his big brother had ditched him for a girl and had broken their promise.

Then Sam was struck with an amazing notion. He had never really thought about moving on before. Life in between—making mischief in Marblehead and playing catch at sundown—had always suited him and Oscar just fine. But Charlie knew best— "Trust me," he liked to say—and if his big brother was willing to risk everything to venture out into the world, then maybe Sam should do the same.

And so, without trumpets or fanfare—without a blinding flash of light or chorus of angels—he had simply crossed over to the next level. The transition was as smooth and effortless as his fast-ball.

His granddad Pop-Pop was there to greet him, along with Barnaby Sweetland, the old caretaker of Waterside, and Florio Ferrente, who delivered a powerful hug and profound apologies for not having saved him in the first place. "Whom the gods love die young," he had said. *"Muor giovane coluiche al cielo è caro."*

From that moment forward, everything had changed for Sam. Gone were a twelve-year-old's preoccupations with kissing girls and playing video games. Vanished were the hurts and pains of a stolen adolescence. Instead, he was filled with the wisdom of the ages and all the knowledge and experience that had eluded him when his life was cut short. With this new perspective, more than ever, Sam wanted to comfort his brother and make sure that everything would be okay.

So he morphed again, this time turning into the giant nimbus formation above the boat. If Charlie had bothered to look up, he would have recognized his brother's face as it emerged in the puffs and curls of the cloud.

Sam could see that his brother was drowned in grief. How could he get him to steer in a new direction? Joe and Tink? Nope, they, too, were locked away—Joe in a wild orgy of spending from a fantasy lottery win, Tink struggling to figure out what he would say to Tess's mother. Sad souls, all of them, Sam thought.

Somehow, someway, Sam knew he had to make Charlie take notice. So he mustered all his strength and shifted shapes once more.

Out of nowhere, a northeasterly wind tousled his bangs, flopping them in his eyes, then back over his head. Abruptly, the air suddenly changed to the southwest, pushing the whitecaps in a new direction. Gulls began to caw. Absorbed in his thoughts, Charlie paid no heed, until a bracing splash of spindrift hit him in the face.

Through stinging eyes, he recognized the sea was in turmoil and the wind was gusting. He jumped to his feet and sprang up the ladder into the tower, where Joe was struggling to stay on course and Tink was studying the charts.

"Need some help?" Charlie offered eagerly.

"Sure," Joe said, "how about driving while I take a leak?"

"No problem."

Charlie seized the wheel and fastened his sight on the white tufts of the waves and their spray, adjusting his steering to every subtle change in the wind's direction. Soon a jagged shape, small and shrouded in gray fog, began to take form in the distance. What was it? A boat? An island?

Suddenly it became clear.

It was an outcropping in the water. Charlie checked the charts. Four hundred yards southeast of Duck Island was Mingo Rock. Through binoculars, he could see its eroded slopes and surface spotted with seaweed and guano. The boat was bouncing now, and he fought to keep his focus on the crag. For an instant, before the boat careened off a wave, he thought he spotted a fleck of color. Doggedly, he repositioned the lenses.

Then he saw something truly extraordinary: a glimpse of orange, the unmistakable color of an ocean survival suit. His heart leaped.

"Look!" he shouted, handing over the binoculars.

"No way," Tink said.

"Holy Mother of God," said Joe, who had just returned to the bridge.

Then Charlie opened the throttle to full speed, the boat roared toward the rock, and three words came to his mouth.

"Don't let go. . . ."

The howling rotors from the Coast Guard Jayhawk blasted Mingo Rock with wind and spray. An aviation survivalman dropped down in a sling on a cable to the ledge where Charlie cradled Tess's head in his lap, her face covered with his jacket to protect her from the downwash. She was still bundled in her survival suit and lashed with a rope to a banged-up watertight aluminum storage container. Her makeshift raft, he guessed: She had probably floated on it until she had found this crag and somehow pulled herself onto it.

His exhilaration had been eviscerated immediately by the reality of her condition. Her skin was almost blue. Her pupils were pinpoint. She had a contusion on the back of her head. She had no detectable pulse.

He had gotten there too late.

His heart was filled with alarm as the survivalman unpacked his emergency kit. The guy didn't waste a word, moving with urgency and efficiency. In this barren spot of gray and cold, Charlie noticed the man's clear blue eyes and pink cheeks. He knew the type. He had trained with them as a paramedic. They were known as airedales, an elite breed. Charlie had always dreamed of joining them and dropping into danger to save lives.

"She's hypothermic," Charlie said. "I've been doing CPR for twenty minutes."

"Good," he said. "We'll take it from here." Deftly, gently, he began to cut Tess from the rope, and Charlie admired his skill. Any sudden movement of the arms and legs of severe hypothermia patients could flood the heart with cold venous blood from the extremities and induce cardiac arrest.

Then the survivalman radioed the helicopter that he was ready, and a rescue hoist litter dropped from the air.

"Where you taking her?" Charlie asked, praying the answer would be a hospital and not the morgue.

"North Shore Emergency. Best hypothermia unit around."

Charlie watched the survivalman lift Tess into the stretcher harness and strap her in. He hooked his belt to the cable, gave the thumbs-up sign to the winch operator, and they lifted off from the rock. Charlie stared straight up into the pounding rotor wake as the basket swayed and was finally pulled inside the helicopter. Then the Jayhawk tilted forward and climbed into the west.

The waves crashed into the rock, and the spray stung his eyes. He watched the orange and white helicopter fade away, and his vision blurred. He was all alone on a rock in the Atlantic, but now he had a shred of hope. He folded his freezing hands, closed his eyes, and prayed to St. Jude.

THIRTY-TWO

CHARLIE HATED THE EMERGENCY ROOM. IT WASN'T LOOK-
ing at these ill and anxious people that unnerved him.
He was uncomfortable because of what he couldn't
see but had always sensed. His gift had never extended
beyond the cemetery gates, but he knew the spirits
were there in the hospital, hovering near their families
or patrolling the long halls. In the land of the living,
the ER was the way station, the earthly equivalent of
the in between.

Was Tess's spirit here now? he wondered, as he sat
on the hard Formica chair and listened to the fish tank
bubbling across from him. Was she floating in the flu-
orescent haze of the waiting room? He closed his eyes
to rest, but his mind would not stop going. He had
spent the last two hours in a frantic, careening race to
the hospital, desperate to get to Tess and find out her

medical status. But no news. The doctors weren't out of the OR yet, and even his old friends on the nursing staff didn't know a thing. Tink sat on the other side of the room. Big fingers poking at his little cell phone, he was dialing numbers all over Marblehead, letting folks know Tess was in the hospital.

Charlie tried to calm himself, but his thoughts kept circling back to the Rule of Three, which had been a fixture of his paramedic training. In desperate situations, people could live for three minutes without oxygen, three hours without warmth, three days without water, three weeks without food. So Tess still had a fighting chance.

He also knew that folks with severe hypothermia often tended to look dead. He reviewed the crucial indicators: hearts slowed, reflexes ceased, bodies stiffened, pulses undetectable, pupils unresponsive. Doctors called this a state of suspended animation or hibernation, the physiological place between life and death. And that was why ER physicians never gave up on exposure victims until they tried to heat the body, blood, and lungs. "You're not dead until you're warm and dead," they liked to say.

In the best-case scenario, Tess was still in between and could be brought back to life, just the way Florio had resuscitated Charlie in the ambulance. The first step was to deliver heated oxygen at a temperature of 107 degrees. The Coast Guard rescuers had surely pumped warm air into her to stabilize heart, lung, and brain temperatures. Next, they would have applied thermo-pads to her head, neck, trunk, and groin to defend her core temperature. Then they would have administered warm fluids through an IV to deal with her severe dehydration.

Once they got her to the hospital, they would have started the delicate job of heating her body to prevent cell damage by adding saline to the stomach, bladder, and lungs or by using a heart-and-lung machine that removed blood from the body, warmed it, and then pumped it back in.

But why were they taking so long in the OR? Maybe it wasn't just hypothermia. Perhaps her head injury was more serious than he imagined. Charlie's thoughts were snapped when the revolving doors spun around and a homeless man lurched through. His shirt was bloody from what Charlie guessed was a gunshot or stab wound in the shoulder.

Then the doors turned again, and Charlie saw Tess's mother enter. He recognized her immediately from the oval shape of her face and the angle of her nose. Charlie jumped up. "Mrs. Carroll," he said, "I'm so sorry I didn't get to Tess sooner."

She shook her head. "Bless you for finding her," she said, reaching out to touch his arm. "Please call me Grace."

"I'm Charlie," he said. "Charlie St. Cloud."

"St. Cloud. Like an angel from the sky," she said. Tink approached and put a burly arm around her.

"Have the doctors told you anything about Tess yet?" Charlie asked.

"No, I got here ten minutes after the helicopter landed, and the Coast Guard wouldn't tell me anything." She stared into Charlie's eyes. "How'd she look when you found her? Was she injured? Did she say anything?"

In that instant, Charlie realized Grace had no idea of the gravity of the situation. He was suddenly thrust back onto Mingo Rock with Tess lying limp in his arms. He had called her name again and again and implored her to wake up. He had told her everyone was waiting in Marblehead for her to come home. But she couldn't hear him. She was gone. No flicker of eyelids, no tremor of lips, no squeeze of the hand.

"I bet Tessie is still talking about sailing around the world this week," Grace was saying through a forced smile.

Before Charlie could answer, the ER doors opened and a nurse came out. It was Sonia Banerji, an old friend from the high-school band. She wore a light blue RN's uniform and her black hair was braided in a long ponytail.

"Mrs. Carroll?" she said. "Please come with me. The doctors are waiting to see you in the back."

"Oh good," Grace said.

Charlie, however, was completely crushed. His stomach clenched. Over the years he had learned to read the signs in the ER. First and foremost, doctors always showed up with good tidings but dispatched the nurses to bring families in when things had gone wrong. Second, families got to see their relatives right away when all was well. They met with the doctors behind closed doors when the news was bad.

"How is Tess?" Grace said. "Please tell me."

"This way please," Sonia said. "The doctors have all the information."

Grace turned to Charlie and said, "Come on, let's go. You, too, Tink. I'm not setting foot in there by myself." The three marched forward into the ER, and Sonia showed them to a private consultation room.

Two young doctors were waiting for them. The first physician began with a few banal pleasantries and introductions. Charlie watched her carefully for clues. Her face expressed compassion, but the muscles in her neck were taut. Her eyes focused intently, but there was a distance to her stare. He recognized the pattern. She was trying to stay detached. That was the way it always was. Doctors and medics couldn't afford to get emotionally involved.

The other M.D. dived into the facts. Her speech was staccato. "Tess suffered acute head trauma and extreme hypothermia. She's in critical condition. She's unable to breathe on her own. We have her on a respirator now."

Grace put her hand to her mouth.

"I can assure you that she isn't in any pain," the doctor said. "She's in a deep coma. She's not responsive in any way. We measure these things on something called the Glasgow Scale. Fifteen is normal. Tess is at level five. It's a very grave situation."

Grace was shaking now, and Tink put his arm around her. "What's going to happen?" he asked. "Will she wake up?"

"No one knows the answer to that question," the doctor said. "She's in God's hands. The only thing we can do is wait."

"Wait for what?" Grace said. "Why can't you do anything?"

"She's a very strong and healthy woman," the doctor said, "and it's quite extraordinary she survived this long. But the cranial trauma was severe, and her exposure to the elements was prolonged." The doctor paused and glanced at her colleague. "There is a theoretical chance her injuries will heal themselves. There are coma cases in the literature that defy explanation. But we believe it's important to be realistic." Her voice lowered. "The likelihood of a reversal is remote."

There was a long silence as the words registered. Charlie felt solid ground collapse beneath him. Then the doctor said, "If you want to have a moment with her, now would be a good time."

THIRTY-THREE

"I QUIT."

They were two words that Charlie never imagined uttering, but he was stunned by how easily they came out. He was standing on the shoulder of Avenue A, the asphalt lane that bisected Waterside. Elihu Swett, the cemetery commissioner, had been making rounds in his Lincoln Continental and had pulled over to the side of the road. From his capacious front seat, he peered up through the open window. "You sure I can't make you reconsider?" Elihu asked.

"I'm sure."

"How about a four percent raise? I think I can get the town to approve that."

"It's not about the money," Charlie said.

"How about another week of vacation? I'm sure I could work that out too."

"No, thanks. It's time to go."

Elihu scowled. "Maybe you'll change your mind," he said, carefully removing the latex glove from his tiny hand and reaching out the window. "You'll always have a place here if you want to come back."

After a good, unprotected shake, Charlie smiled. "I hope it's a long time before they bring me here." Then he jumped into his cart and scooted off along the paths, stopping to adjust a sprinkler head or to clip back branches in a pyramid hedge. The flowers seemed more radiant, the inscriptions on even the most ancient memorials seemed more distinct, as if someone had turned on the lights.

It was Friday, the day of the week to work on monuments. The gang was in the field scrubbing and fixing the gravestones. There were 52,434 of them in Waterside, and they came in every shape and size. Marble from Italy. Granite from Vermont. Literally, millions and millions of dollars spent on rock and remembering. Someday, Charlie hoped to be remembered too. For being a good brother. For finding Tess. For doing something with his life.

He had decided to treat his last day like every other, so he did his chores, made his rounds, and stopped to say good-bye to his pals. Joe the Atheist hugged him hard and confided that he was rethinking his relationship to God. The *Horny Toad*, he added, was available at any hour for a damsel in distress. Near the fountain, Charlie ran into Bella Hooper, The Woman Who Listens. "Everyone's talking about what you did," she said. "You know, going out there and finding Tess. Never giving up. It's amazing. You're the new hero in town."

"Thanks, Bella, but it was no big deal."

"We should talk about that sometime," she said. "I'm available whenever you want. Special friends-and-family rate."

He zoomed around the grounds for the last time, satisfied with how serene and groomed the cemetery looked. Then, back in the cottage, he threw his few good things into a duffel bag, packed his favorite books and tapes in another, folded his blue Waterside shirts and left them on the dresser, wiped some dishes dry, and took out the trash. He would leave the inherited furniture from Barnaby Sweetland for the next caretaker. He looped the keys on the hook, set his bags out on the step, and closed the door behind him. Then he loaded the cart and headed north.

He took the turns by heart, right, left, half circle around the lake, and from there he drove toward the small mausoleum on the hill shaded by two willow trees. The specks in the marble sparkled, and the pair of carved baseball bats made it seem grand. Lichen had grown around the name chiseled on the lintel:

ST. CLOUD

He got out of the cart, took an old-fashioned skeleton key from the glove compartment, and opened the door. In the semi-darkness, he sat on the little sarcophagus and swung his legs. He chucked the ball into the mitt. Then, with a smile at the blue angel in the stained-glass window, he put them down on the smooth Carrara marble. Right where they belonged.

The sun was going down, and Charlie knew it was time to go. He locked the vault and stood looking down on the harbor below. God, he would miss Sam and their mischief. Then the wind picked up, the trees in the forest began to shudder, and a flurry of crimson oak leaves floated down, twirled in front of him, and blew away.

Sam was there, Charlie knew right away. His brother was all around him in the air, the sky, the sunset, and the leaves. Those games of boyhood catch were best left in his memory. But he couldn't resist. On his last day at Waterside, there was one more place to go.

THIRTY-FOUR

THE HIDDEN PLAYGROUND WAS SILENT. NO FUSSING BIRDS, no frantic squirrels, no spirits drifting. It was 6:51 P.M.

Charlie paced from the dirt mound to home plate and then back again. He wanted to remember every inch—the cedar grove, the swing, the bench. Where was Sam now, he wondered. What he wouldn't give to have his kid brother stop by for one final farewell.

Charlie drank in the sylvan setting, memorizing the color of the leaves and the angles of the light. He knew he would never return again to this crepuscular realm, and soon the clearing itself would be gone. The forest would overrun the ball field, and no one would even know it had ever existed.

The thought brought tears to his eyes. This had been the most important space in the world to him, but he had made his choice and now there was somewhere else he needed to be. He took a deep breath, inhaling the musty fragrance of autumn, and was about to go when he was startled to see a young man walking across the grass. At first, he wondered who else had discovered the hidden playground. In thirteen years, no one had ever penetrated this sanctuary.

The intruder was tall, at least 6'3", and his shoulders were square and broad. His face was narrow and long, his hair was curly, and his shining eyes were unmistakable.

Charlie gasped in astonishment.

It was Sam.

"Hey, big bro," he said with a smile.

Charlie couldn't speak. Gone were his brother's Sox cap, baggy shorts, and high-tops. He was wearing a bomber jacket, jeans, and boots.

"Look at you!" Charlie said.

"What?"

"You're a man."

"Yes," he said, "I'm finally a man and I can do what I want."

They were face-to-face now, and Charlie realized that his brother was glimmering like a hologram with luminous surfaces. Sam was now a reflection of the past and the present and a projection of the future—all he had been and all he wanted to be.

Charlie threw his arms around his brother's evanescing shape and was stunned that they couldn't touch. His grasp held nothing. Sam was no longer in between. He was ether now, but Charlie could still feel his warmth and the strength of the connection.

"You crossed over," he said.

"I did."

"And how is it?"

"Beyond anything we ever imagined, Charlie. It's mind-blowing. You'll see."

"So how did you get back here? I didn't realize you could return."

"There are lots of things you don't understand," Sam said. "But don't worry. That's the way it's supposed to be."

Then they wandered into the forest, sat on the log by the pond where the catfish and sunnies hid from the great blue heron, and told each other about the last few days.

"You mad I broke the promise?" Charlie asked.

"No," Sam said. "It was time. We were holding each other back."

In that moment, Charlie realized what he had truly lost in those thirteen years. They had never shared an adult conversation. Sam had not grown up, and their relationship had been frozen in time.

Charlie wished he could wrap his arm around Sam's shoulders. "That was you out there on the water the other morning, wasn't it?" he asked. "You know, with the spray and the wind?"

"Sure took you long enough to notice!"

"What can I say? Negligence in the first degree. Guilty as charged."

"Negligence, noun," Sam said, starting to smile. "The sexy nightgown a girl forgets she's wearing when she goes to work in the morning." He laughed and slapped his knee, and Charlie roared. He studied the translucent outlines of his brother who had grown so much and yet was still the same.

"I guess I have only one regret," Charlie said. "I'm sorry I held on to you for so long." He wiped tears from his face.

"It's okay," Sam said. "I held on just as much as you."

There was a long silence, then Charlie asked, "You think we'll ever play catch again?"

"Of course," Sam said. "We'll be back together in the blink of an eye. And then we'll have forever."

"Promise you won't leave me," Charlie said.

"Promise."

"Swear?" he said, amazed to find himself repeating the very same conversation from all those years ago. This time, however, it was Sam who comforted Charlie.

"I swear," his kid brother said.

"Cross your heart and hope to die?"

"Hope to die," Sam said. "I love you."

"I love you too." The brothers stood up.

Sam went to the larch tree at the foot of the pond. There was a thick, knotted rope hanging from a lower branch. "One last push?" he said.

With a whoop, Charlie pushed, and Sam began to swing out over the water. "Bye, big bro," he shouted, letting go and reaching for the sky. He tucked into a tight forward somersault with a twist. Gone were the gangly arms and legs, and Charlie felt blessed that just once he had seen him in all his glory.

Then Sam was gone, vanished, and the clearing was absolutely silent except for the swinging rope and a flurry of crimson oak leaves on the wind.

THIRTY-FIVE

THE LAST CLOSING TIME, THE LAST ZOOM AROUND TO collect an elderly gentleman in a seersucker suit on the Vale of Serenity.

"Evening," Charlie said.

Palmer Guidry's hair was wavy and white, and as he poured the last drop from his red watering can, his old cassette recorder played Brahms.

"Well, hello, Charles!"

"We're shutting down for the night. Can I give you a lift?"

"Why, thank you. So good of you."

Mr. Guidry folded his dust rag, switched off the tape player, and made a final inspection of the crimson bloom of a tall plant.

"Hollyhocks were Betty's favorite," he said.

"I think you told me once."

"You know, Betty planted the whole backyard with pink holly-hocks one time. They grew seven feet high!"

"Oh really?"

He climbed into the cart and tucked the watering can under his legs.

"Night, Betty," he said. "Sweet dreams, my love. Be back soon."

"Want to come over for dinner tonight?" Mr. Guidry said as they approached the iron gates. "I'll whip up one of Betty's favorites. Finest meat loaf on God's green earth."

"Yes," Charlie said. "I'd like that. In fact, I'd like that a lot."

Mr. Guidry hesitated for a moment. Even with Alzheimer's he knew something was different. Something had changed. Something wonderful. His eyes twinkled, and his face displayed a hint of recognition. "Don't you have someplace to be?" he asked. "Isn't that what you always say?" It was another little miracle, one of those mysterious moments of clarity in a confusing world.

"Not anymore," Charlie said. "I'll follow you home. Just don't drive too fast."

"I'm at Cow Corners on Guernsey and Jersey," Mr. Guidry said. "It's the old gray house with green shutters."

"Gotcha."

As Charlie pushed the great iron gates shut for the last time, he smiled at the ancient, creaking sound. Someone else would get to squirt oil on those giant hinges. Now he stood on the out-side and peered through the metal grille across the cemetery where the willows bowed toward the lake, the fountain was quiet, and not a soul stirred.

He let go of the iron bars, turned and hefted his two duffels into the back of his Rambler. Mr. Guidry pulled out onto West Shore Drive in his Buick, and Charlie followed him down the street that skirted the edge of the cemetery. He looked out the window and waved good-bye to the rows of monuments, the acres of lawns, and his world within a world. And Charlie St. Cloud, dearly departed caretaker of Waterside Cemetery, never looked back.

THIRTY-SIX

MARBLEHEAD HUMMED WITH THANKSGIVING WEEK CONtentment. The chilly air carried the comforting scent of burning logs. Hibernating boats huddled on winter dry docks and dreamed of warm weather. Twinkling Christmas decorations made their merry debut. Around Engine Company 2 on Franklin Street, life was especially good. There hadn't been a big blaze since the School Street Fire.

Charlie was wearing the uniform of a full-time paramedic at the station, now also his home until he found a place of his own. On this utterly uneventful Friday, as the clock in the rec room chimed six—time for a shift change—Charlie grabbed a coat from his locker and headed out to the Rambler. With a few extra turns of the key, he brought the old car to life. Sure, it was almost ready for the scrap yard, but it was a good ride, and sometimes he could drive all day and late into the night just to feel the road rushing beneath him.

Tonight Charlie had only one place to go. He headed down Pleasant Street, veered onto MA-114 toward Salem, and within minutes pulled into the parking lot of the North Shore Medical Center. He walked right through the lobby, waved to the admission nurses, and went straight to Room 172. He knocked gently, then opened the door.

Tess was alone and asleep in her coma. Bandages and ventilator gone, she was pale, but was breathing on her own now. Her hands were folded on her chest, and she seemed completely at peace. He had memorized every single detail of her oval face, her pale lips, and her long eyelashes. It was so strange. He had touched every inch of her that night in the cottage, and yet he didn't know her physically at all.

In eight weeks, Charlie had studied all sorts of books and articles on brain injury. The longest, best-documented complete recovery from a coma was two and a half years, but he had uncovered even more-amazing cases, like the Albuquerque woman who had arisen from a sixteen-year sleep one Christmas day and had asked to go shopping at the mall, and the fifty-three-year-old Toronto shopkeeper who had fallen into a coma and had awoken thirty years later wondering, "What's on TV?"

Those were the extreme examples, but he knew something miraculous could also happen for Tess, and, in a way, it already had. God had answered his prayers. She hadn't vanished from the cemetery because she was moving on to the next realm. She had disappeared because she was trying to return to this life.

He had spent so many hours here by her bedside in this room

that had been made homey by Grace and her friends. There were plants from Kipp's Greenhouses and get-well cards from Mrs. Paternina's science class. Hanging over her bed, an autographed poster of Tom Brady, the Patriots quarterback and Super Bowl hero, said, *Get well soon.* Photos of her dad fishing on his lobster boat and of *Querencia* in sea trials crowded the bedside table.

"Big weekend for your boys," Charlie said, sitting down beside her. He pulled *The Boston Globe* sports page from his coat pocket and read her the highlights. "Looks like the Jets plan to challenge your linebackers with some new tight end they drafted."

This was Charlie's ritual now, but he was nonetheless watchful that he not slip back into his old habit of following a fixed routine. Sometimes he stopped by in the morning. On other occasions he dropped by after work. One week he would skip a few days, then another he would show up steadily for a stretch.

He wanted to be there for her, but he also wanted to live his life. He had picked up tickets for a New Year's trip to the Pacific Northwest to see his mother. And he was planning a backpacking adventure across Africa and Asia a year from now.

With each visit, Charlie always gave Tess the latest. Today he shared the delicious new scandal in town. Reverend Polkinghorne had been caught naked on the dock of the Eastern Yacht Club with two—yes, two—of his flock: Sherry Trench and Gena Carruthers.

Charlie believed Tess was listening to every word of every story. He tried to make things quick and funny. He wanted to charm her, even in her sleep. Sometimes he imagined her throwing her head back in laughter. Other times he pictured her giving him grief when he went on too long.

When he was tired of talking, he went to the window to watch the sun go down. "It's gorgeous tonight," he said. "You ought to see it." He still felt that alarm inside warn him that he needed to be in the forest. But then he saw the moon rising and he knew Sam was still out there.

It was dark now. The hospital was silent. It was time to go. "Night, Tess," he said. "I sure miss you." He kissed her on the cheek and had started through the door when he realized he had forgotten to say something. "I'm having dinner with Tink tonight," he said, going back to her. "We're heading over to the Barnacle. I wish you warned me how much that guy could eat. There aren't enough clams in the ocean to fill him up." He reached forward and pushed her bangs away.

Then Charlie saw her lashes flutter and her incredible emerald eyes open, and he wondered if he was imagining them.

THIRTY-SEVEN

MIST SHROUDED THE GROUND, MUFFLING THE SOUNDS OF the world. She couldn't see anyone else around. She could have been anywhere or nowhere. It didn't matter. Charlie was gone, her father had never come to greet her, and she was all alone.

Ever since leaving the cemetery, she had been in this same place. It was like the deep ocean on a moonless night. The sky was a blanket of black without familiar stars to give her bearings. In the distance, vague shapes like thunderheads seemed to shift about. Sometimes voices emerged around her, then went away.

She had tried to call for help but no one answered. She wanted to cut through the gloom but couldn't seem to budge. And so she had waited, watching for the moment to make her move.

Now was the time.

At first, with darkness slowly giving way to light, everything was blurry. Her brain, the room, and the man looking down at her. "Tess," he kept saying. "Tess, can you hear me?" Of course she could hear him. She wanted to form words in response, but she couldn't make sounds. How strange. She tried again, but her mouth and throat were parched. When at last she found her voice, it was raspy and barely audible. "Tess," she said. "Tess."

"Yes, Tess!" the man said. He was so excited.

"Yes, Tess," she repeated.

"You're back! My God, you're back!"

"You're back," she said. She knew she was just repeating his words, but it was the best she could do.

"How do you feel?" he was saying. "Does anything hurt?"

In fact, she couldn't feel a thing. Her body was numb and her head groggy. She moved her eyes around the room. "Where?" she began tentatively. "Where am I?" That wasn't bad, she thought. *Where am I?* A complete sentence. She smiled faintly, and the skin on her cheeks felt tight.

"You're in the hospital," he said. "North Shore Medical Center in Salem."

The words didn't register entirely. "Where?" she said again.

"The hospital. You had an accident. You were injured. But everything's okay now."

Hospital. Accident. Injured.

"What accident?" she said.

"You were sailing," he said. "Your boat caught fire in a storm. Do you remember?"

Fire. Storm. She didn't recall a thing. "Boat," she said. "What happened?"

"It was destroyed," he said. "I'm sorry, but *Querencia* burned and sank."

Querencia. She liked the way that sounded, and the lilt of the syllables brought back fragments of memory and meaning. "*Querencia.* Spanish, safe place."

"Yes!" the man said. "You're right. It's Spanish."

She was trying to focus. More thoughts were taking shape.

"Water," she said. "I'm thirsty."

The man hurried to the sink and poured her a glass. Gently, he held it to her lips, and she took a sip, swirling the cool liquid in her mouth. She squinted toward the window, where the branches of a tree were blowing in the wind. "Window," she said.

"Yes, window."

"Open it, please."

The man rushed over, threw the bolt, and slid it up. "There you go."

An amazing breeze wafted into the room, and Tess closed her eyes as it rustled her hair and soothed her. Water and wind. Yes, she loved them both.

The man reached for the phone. "I'm calling your mom. Okay?"

"Okay," she said. "Mom."

The man punched the numbers and began to speak rapidly. She couldn't follow what he was saying. When he put it down, she asked, "Who are you? Doctor?"

"It's me, Charlie. Remember?"

She didn't remember. Her memory was blank.

"Tess, please, try to think back," he was saying. "It's me, Charlie."

She shook her head. "I'm sorry, I just don't remember..." Then she saw tears streaming down his face. Why was he crying? "What's wrong?" she said.

"Nothing's wrong. I'm just so happy to see you."

Tess smiled, and this time her face didn't feel so taut. "Your name?" she said. "What's your name?"

"Charlie St. Cloud."

Charlie St. Cloud. She crinkled her nose. Things were coming back faster now. Files were opening in her brain. "St. Cloud," she said. "Not a Marblehead name."

"You're right," he answered. "Minnesota. Long story too."

"I like stories," she said.

And then Charlie sat down beside her and explained how his name came from a Mississippi River town where his mother had grown up. The original St. Cloud was a sixth-century French prince who renounced the world to serve God after his brothers were murdered by an evil uncle.

Tess liked the deep timbre of his voice. It reminded her of someone but she couldn't place it. When he was done telling her the story, she reached out and touched his hand. It felt so warm and strong.

"The Patriots have a big game this weekend," he was saying. "You love football, remember?" She studied his gentle face with a dimple in one cheek. There was something different about this man.

"Tell me another story, Charlie."

"Anything you want," he said, and he began to talk of sailing around the world to distant places like the Marquesas, Tuamotu Islands, Tonga, and Fiji.

Every word came like comfort, so she eased back into the pillows and basked in the warmth of Charlie's caramel eyes. Slowly, her edges began to soften, and she wondered how she already knew that she could listen to this man for a very long time.

It was past midnight.

The doctors had finished checking Tess and, incredibly, had determined that her physical and cognitive functions were intact, and her memory would likely return to normal.

A writer and photographer from the *Reporter* had rushed over to ask questions and snap pictures for a special edition of the paper. Tink and the crew from the sail loft had paraded through with encouragement and news from the company. Her joy exceeding her energy, Grace had finally gone to sleep on a pullout cot in the next room.

Now all was quiet.

Wide awake in the waiting room, Charlie stared at the fish tank with its neon tetras darting back and forth. Grateful as he was that she was back, his mind stuck on one question: Would she remember him?

Their first kiss . . .

Their night in each other's arms . . .

As friends and family surrounded her that evening, Charlie had watched as she gradually recalled *Querencia*'s struggle against the storm. She had even started planning her next solo race around the world, calculating that it would take one year to outfit a new boat and to train properly. Whenever her gaze turned to Charlie in the back of the room—and it was often—she had smiled but seemed unsure who he was or why he was there.

Who could blame her?

The doors opened across the waiting room, and a nurse beckoned in a hushed voice, "She's asking for you, Charlie."

"What?"

"She wants to see you."

He covered the distance to her bedside in what seemed like five steps. Amazingly, she was sitting up, her face softly illuminated by the night-light. "I'm glad you're still here," she said.

"I'm glad you are too," Charlie answered.

She was studying him intensely. Finally she said, "So you're the one who found me."

"I guess that's true."

"After everyone had given up?"

"Pretty much."

"I need to know something," she said. "It's important."

"Yes, I confess, I'm a Red Sox fan," he said with a smile.

She threw her head back and laughed. "I can forgive that," she said, "but there's one thing I can't remember."

"What's that?"

"How we met."

"You wouldn't believe me if I told you."

"Try me," she said. "Tell me our story."

"Well," he recalled, "it starts in Waterside Cemetery where a brave and beautiful sailmaker complained to the caretaker about a disturbance of the peace." Charlie smiled. "The charming fellow tried to explain the importance of his geese-management program, but the unimpressed sailor only laughed."

And so Charlie tenderly described their first encounters from a candlelit dinner with a Ted Williams cake to a midnight walk with weeping willows and a marble mausoleum. As her eyes registered every detail, he was filled with hope. He had let go of the past and reclaimed his life. And now, the greatest blessing of all, he and Tess were starting over.

AFTERWORD

I BELIEVE IN MIRACLES, AND NOW YOU KNOW WHY.

I stand on a sloping hill in Waterside Cemetery, a place Charlie loved and shaped with his own hands. The seagulls fly in force. The iron gates stand open. A girl hangs upside down from an oak. A fuzzy old man puts a fistful of hollyhocks on his wife's grave.

That's the world you know. It's the one you can see when you pass by the cemetery in your town. It's the one that's real and reassuring. But there's another world here too. I'm talking about what you and Charlie can't see yet, the level beyond the in between. It's a place called heaven, paradise, or nirvana—they're all the same, really—and it's where I came when I crossed over. It's where Mrs. Ruth Phipps can once again hold hands with her beloved Walter. It's where Barnaby Sweetland, the old caretaker of

Waterside, can sing with the angels. And of course, it's where Sam and Oscar can explore the universe.

From this vantage point, I see everything now. My voice and thoughts are wind, and I send them toward Charlie. He's with Tess in North Shore Medical, where she gets stronger every day.

Yes, that's one of our abilities on this side—to glimpse, hear, and know all. We are everywhere. We experience everything. We rejoice when you rejoice. We're sad when you're sad. We grieve when you grieve. And when you hold on too long, it hurts us the same way it hurts you. I think of my wife, Francesca, and our son. I know it will take time and many tears, but I want them to move on. Someday she'll marry again and find new happiness.

There's Charlie now, making his way from the hospital to Logan Airport. He's going to visit his mother in Oregon. He'll tell her what he has learned living in the twilight and he'll explain how much of himself he lost after the accident. For all his efforts, his mom will never understand. She moved across the country, started a new life, and hoped to bury the accident in the past. But in the quiet moments of her days and nights, she can never escape that her younger son was taken too soon, and it's always too soon. She will never recover.

That is the inescapable math of tragedy and the multiplication of grief. Too many good people die a little when they lose someone they love. One death begets two or twenty or one hundred. It's the same all over the world.

Charlie will understand that it's his mother's choice whether to hold on or let go. You know that Charlie has chosen to live. After staying with his mom for a while, he'll come back to Marblehead and work with Engine Company 2 on Franklin

Street. He'll travel around the world. Most of all, he'll make up for thirteen lost years and dive for dreams.

I'm reminded of Ecclesiastes and something I once told Charlie: "The Bible got it wrong. There isn't time in a man's life for everything."

That's right. Charlie doesn't have time. No one does. But he knows what's important now. First and foremost, he and Tess will fall in love again. They'll kiss for the first time. They'll sail the coral cays of Belize on their honeymoon. They'll settle down on Cloutman's Lane in the same house where he grew up. They'll have two sons. For the first time in forever, he'll wake up to a new beagle's bark every morning, with a feeling that the world is all right and everyone he cares about is safe and sound. He'll build his boys a playground with swings under a pine tree. He'll play a good game of catch with them every night, and he'll encourage them to race the moon and go on great adventures.

Charlie's gift of seeing the spirit world faded away just as soon as he and Sam released each other for the last time. But every day, he'll try to live with his eyes open to the other side, letting the possibility of miracles in. Sometimes he'll forget, but then he'll see a rope swinging on a pond, catch the Sox on the radio, or hear a dog yowl. He'll know Oscar and Sam are there.

That's death and life, you see. We all shine on. You just have to release your hearts, alert your senses, and pay attention. A leaf, a star, a song, a laugh. Notice the little things, because somebody is reaching out to you. *Qualcuno ti ama.* Somebody loves you.

And one day—only God knows precisely when—Charlie will run out of time. He'll be an old man, floppy hair turned gray. He'll look back on his quietly remarkable life and know he made good on his promise. And then, like the 75 billion souls who lived before him, each and every one a treasure, he, too, will die.

When that day comes, we'll be waiting. Waiting for Charlie St. Cloud to come home to us. Until then we offer these parting words...

May he live in peace.

A NOTE ON SOURCES

THE SETTINGS IN THIS STORY ARE REAL, AND I AM GRATE-
ful to many good folks in Marblehead, Massachusetts,
for welcoming me to their town. Special thanks to
F. Emerson Welch of the *Reporter* for fielding questions with Fraffian wit and cheer from dawn to dusk;
Bump Wilcox of New Wave Yachts for steering a land-
lubber through imaginary Force 10 storms and the
crew of *Loonatic* for a bruising victory in the Wednesday night races; and Kristen Heissenbuttel at Doyle
Sailmakers for revealing the art and science of sail design. Appreciation also goes to Harbormaster Warner
Hazell and his deputies; Bette Hunt and the
Marblehead Historical Society; Commodore B. B.
Crowninshield of the CBYC and Lynn Marine Supply;
the firefighters of Engine 2 on Franklin Street; Ed
Cataldo of Engine 5 in Revere; Todd Basch and Carol

Wales of Doyle Sails; Marjorie Slattery-Sumner; Sheila Duncan (the original Woman Who Listens); Sally and Roger Plauché of Spray Cliff on the Ocean; Ruth and Skip Sigler of the Seagull Inn; Suzanne and Peter Conway of the Harbor Light Inn; and the regulars at the Barnacle, Driftwood, Landing, Maddie's, and Rip Tide. At the U.S. Coast Guard in Boston and Gloucester, a salute to Chief Petty Officers Steven Carriere, Tim Hudson, and Paul Wells, and Petty Officer Jared Coon for explaining search and rescue operations. At the Beverly Hills Fire Department, thanks to former Deputy Chief Mike Smollen for help with Hurst tools and Zoll defibrillators.

The bulk of this book unfolds in Waterside Cemetery, where Headers will recognize I took liberties with the landscape. Many thanks go to Superintendent Bill James and his longtime predecessor Ben Woodfin. For the most unusual week of work and research in my life, I am indebted to John Toale Jr., Steven Sloane, Don Williams, and Susan Olsen of historic Woodlawn Cemetery in Bronx, New York. Without hesitation, they sent me out to mow lawns and carry caskets on their 400 acres. I thank the foremen, union shop stewards, and workers for always giving me a hand and going easy when my back was breaking. A special tip of my blue Woodlawn cap to grave diggers Bob Blackmore, Greg Link, and Ray Vicens for sharing the finer points of their craft and the daily gratuities. Appreciation also goes to Ken Taylor of Green-Wood Cemetery in Brooklyn, New York, for insights based on more than thirty-five years of working and living with the dead.

For illuminating the afterlife, I offer gratitude to the incomparable Rosemary Altea, spirit medium and friend. Her bestselling books, including *The Eagle and the Rose* and *Proud Spirit,* are marvels of insight and meaning. Along the way I learned much from many other works, including Peter Canning's *Rescue 471*; Linda Greenlaw's *The Hungry Ocean* and *Lobster Chronicles*; Thomas Lynch's *The Undertaking*; Sherwin B. Nuland's *How We Die*; Elisabeth Kübler-Ross's *On Death and Dying*; John Rousmaniere's *Fastnet, Force 10*; and Studs Terkel's *Will the Circle Be Unbroken?* On the Internet, I turned often to the *Marblehead Reporter*; *Marblehead Magazine*; Griefnet; Beyond Indigo; and City of the Silent, the remarkable cemetery website. For Sam and Charlie's wordplay, I drew on *The Washington Post*'s "Style Invitational" of May 1998 asking readers to redefine words from the dictionary. For Florio's reflections on Ecclesiastes, I was inspired by Yehuda Amichai's poem, "A Man in His Life."

For a photo tour of the settings in this story and more information on sources, please visit www.bensherwood.com.

ACKNOWLEDGMENTS

THIS BOOK IS ABOUT SECOND CHANCES, AND I'M GRATE-ful to many friends and colleagues for helping with mine. Thanks go first to my far-flung writing pals. Alan Levy, cyber officemate, was there every day with bold ideas, humor, and encouragement; Barry Edelstein gave the gifts of uncommon friendship, intelligence, and dramaturgy; Maxine Paetro counseled with her exalted perspective and flair; Akiva Goldsman showed how to break out of the box; Gary Ross asked impossible questions; John Bowe reminded if it isn't hard, it isn't worth it; and Bruce Feiler guided with brilliant strategy and tactics and led the way to greater meaning with his penetrating mind and work. Gratitude also to J. J. Abrams, Bob Dolman, and Stan Pottinger.

Profound appreciation to friends who read at many

stages: Rebecca Ascher-Walsh, David Doss, Lynn Harris, Joannie Kaplan, Steve Kehela, Christy Prunier, Kim Roth, Jennifer Sherwood, and Jamie Tarses.

Once more, I am privileged to be published by the Bantam family. Publisher Irwyn Applebaum and Senior Editor Danielle Perez deserve medals of valor for seeing Charlie St. Cloud through his unruly childhood and disobedient adolescence and for their unwavering care in helping find the story I meant to write from the beginning. Special commendations to Barb Burg and Susan Corcoran, friends, psychologists, and advocates.

At Picador in Britain, fistfuls of flowers to Ursula Doyle, Stephanie Sweeney, and Candice Voysey. In Los Angeles, an ovation to Marc Platt and Abby Wolf-Weiss for imagining Charlie St. Cloud on the silver screen, and to Donna Langley at Universal Pictures for being the book's champion.

Pages and pages of appreciation go to Joni Evans, supreme friend, coconspirator, and agent, who enriched every draft, deflected every bullet, and makes diving for dreams a reality. Boldface credit also to Alicia Gordon, Tracy Fisher, Andy McNiccol, Michelle Bohan, and Mike Sheresky.

Great gratitude goes to friends who aided and abetted along the way: Jonathan Barzilay; Jane and Marcus Buckingham; Chrissy, Priscilla, and Norm Colvin; Beth de Guzman; Sara Demenkoff; Debby Goldberg; Meg Greengold; Cindy Guidry; Suzy Landa; Ruth Jaffe; Mary Jordan; Barry Rosenfeld; Julie and Mark Rowen; Melissa Thomas; and Joe Torsella. A bow to David Segal for expert music recommendations. Dov Seidman, entrepreneur and chess adversary, deserves special recognition for urging a deeper investment. SPF-15 to Kristin Mannion and H. P.

Goldfield for Whimsea. And a kiss to the late Phyllis Levy, who helped inspire this book and watches over from above.

Now a few words to my family. Once more, my mother, Dorothy Sherwood, attacked the manuscript with her relentless pencil and exacting standards, chomping on every word. Her talent as an editor is surpassed only by her genius as a parent. Jeffrey Randall, my generous and indefatigable neurosurgeon brother-in-law, kept the twenty-four-hour medical hotline open for every sort of professional and personal emergency. Someday my young nephews Richard and William Randall will read this story, and I wish them a sibling bond as rich, strong, and sustaining as the one I share with their accomplished and exceptional mother—my shining sister—Elizabeth Sherwood Randall. Our connection, forged in countless childhood adventures, informed much of this book, as did the memory of our father, Richard Sherwood, who vanished too soon but whose presence we feel every day.

Finally, this novel is dedicated to my wife, Karen Kehela Sherwood, whose heart, mind, and rare storytelling gifts grace every page. She is my *querencia*—my sunny spot, safe harbor, and true love.